His Protection

His Guardians Book 8

By

Ronna Bacon

ISBN 978-1-989000-26-7
Library and Archives Canada

Verses to Remember

Psalms 46:1. God is our refuge and strength, an ever-present help in trouble.

Psalm 121:1, 2.   I lift my eyes to the mountains - where does my help come from? My help comes from the Lord, the maker of heaven and earth.

Psalms 91: 14, 15. "Because he loves me," says the Lord, "I will rescue him; I will protect him, for he acknowledges my name. He will call on me, and I will answer him' I will be with him in trouble, I will deliver him and honour him.

Table of Contents

He watched from the doorway as she packed her belongings, not letting her see him. He couldn't let her leave. She had that money he wanted, and she would turn it over to him.

As she walked down the stairs, he approached her. "Have a meal with me, please?"

She shook her head. "Not happening. I'm out of here."

He reached to stop her. "Then at least have a cup of tea with me. If you're leaving, then let us part as friends."

She stared at him, then abruptly nodded, not wanting to spend any more time with this man, who she didn't trust. She felt evil around him and wondered how her aunt had ever seen anything in him.

Ten minutes later, he stared down at her as she lay unconscious on the floor. The drugs had worked. He lifted her and carried her back to her bedroom, shutting and locking the door behind him as he left. He had plans to put in place now. She would not defeat him; he would defeat her.

The younger man standing in the shadows searched the face of his employer, then turned to the locked door. Somehow, he would free her from this monster. He had planned to run away himself that day, but he decided to stay. This young woman, who had been kind to him, needed his help.

Chapter 1

Staring at the building in front of him, Abe Finlay tapped his fingers on the steering wheel of his SUV, not sure if he was taking the right step. His team, Rebel's Elite Security, had taken hit after hit with his men and their ladies over the last months, but now each of his men had married the women they loved. He knew he had to try this, to find the woman he still loved, but who had disappeared on him. Maybe Tracker's would be the one to find her for him. He sighed, then looked back at the road behind him. He was torn. Lord, what do I do? Do I go on as I have, living a solitary life, with my friends and family questioning me as to who I am going to find to love, just like they have, or do I enter that building and talk to Jace or even Tracker herself? He had felt peace at home when he had set out. Now, the doubts were rising within him.

He slid from behind the wheel and shut the door, still reluctant to move forward. Hand on the door, he paused, then prayed.

Finding the confidence he needed, he walked towards the office and entered through a plain steel door. Nothing fancy about this building, he thought, but they do certainly come through when we need them.

He stopped in the reception area, noting the cream wallpaper, the dark wood trim, and the dark oak flooring under his feet. Tapestry-covered chairs sat around. He walked over to take a look at a picture of an eagle hanging on the wall.

He turned once more as he heard a woman's voice. He tilted his head. It was so familiar, but it couldn't be her, could it? He walked over towards the reception desk and stared at the woman standing with her back to him, talking to Jace. Russet hair in a ponytail teased his memories.

"Emma?" Abe's voice was barely audible. Surely, after all these years, it wouldn't be so easy. "Emma, is that you?"

Tracker froze. No one called her Emma, not any more. The only one she wanted to call her by that name was dead. Her aunt's husband had assured her of that, showing her the paperwork.

Jace watched as Abe once again called Tracker Emma, walking towards her as he spoke, stopping just feet from her. Her fingers on her mouth, her eyes slid shut as tears traced down her face. He saw the rigid self-control she always held herself under start to crack and the inscrutable look on her face fade.

"Emma?" Abe's voice was hesitant. He still wasn't sure it was her, the one who had stolen his heart so many years ago.

Emma turned, hardly able to see for the tears. "Abe! He told me you were dead! Oh, Abe, what did he do?"

Abe moved forward, stopped just short of touching her. He reached to touch her cheek, tracing the track of the tears. Then, he reached, drawing her into his arms.

"I'm not dead, my darling." He wrapped her as tight as he could in his arms. She clung to him as sobs wracked her body. "He told me you wanted nothing more to do with me."

Jace watched, then turned and walked out the back door of the building. He wasn't needed. He now knew whose memory it was that Emma (he was having difficulty with that name) had clung to all those years. As her friend, he had tried to help find him, but she refused to talk about it.

Finally, Emma's sobs stopped, and she leaned back to look up at Abe's face. She reached to touch his own tear-streaked face. "Oh, Abe. What happened? What did he do to us?"

"You know who it was?"

She nodded. "Auntie Em's third husband. I had something he wanted, as you know, and there is still something he wants, those trust fund monies."

Abe nodded as he searched the face of the woman he hadn't stopped loving. "Then, let's find him and stop this. We need to figure out where we stand and what we want to do." He reached for her hand. "Come, let's go."

She shook her head. "No, Abe. We need to be cautious. We have to make plans first before we do or say anything." She broke free of him and began to pace. "We need somewhere neutral we can meet, someone who can help us if we need help."

Abe nodded at her wisdom. "Then, let's think about it then." He turned to pace. "I have it. It would not be strange for me to visit my uncle Eddie. I can get his wife to invite you over in the evenings on some pretext."

She shook her head, and he placed his hand on her face. "It will work, Emma. Eddie knows your name, he saw the condition I was left in by that man, and he has tried for years to help."

She finally nodded. "Set it up, then, Abe." She looked around the business office. "Jace was here. He and his family were a Godsend to me all those years ago. He has never pried, but I think he knows part of the story."

Abe reached once more for the woman he loved. Cradling her in his arms, he prayed for them both, asking for God's protection and wisdom as to the decisions they needed to make and the plans they needed to set into place. He was determined that he would find the man responsible and bring him to justice.

Emma stepped back. "You need to go now, Abe. I need some time just to absorb the fact that you're not really dead after all." She studied his face, then nodded. "I have a thick file of material on Charlie already. Let me know when you have a day set up, and I'll bring you copies." She paused, then looked back up at him. "I guess I'll need to give Eddie a copy as well."

"That would be good. He can get started on this. He's been itching for years to get his hands on Charlie, but I've never given him a name to work with."

Abe paused before he slid behind the wheel, staring at the office building. Lord, You knew she was here all along. You have prepared me for today, with what my guys have gone through. Lead us, Lord. We'll need Your protection. With one last glance at the building, he slid behind the wheel and set off to find his uncle, not sure if he would be at the police department where he was the lead detective or at home. Pulling to the side of the road, he dialed Eddie's number. Assured that he was at home, Abe headed that way, heart in mouth, to finally share with Eddie what had happened all those years ago. He wasn't sure how Eddie would take it. He shook his head. To think that his Emma had been here and that his guys had worked with her. He smiled, anticipating telling them.

Chapter 2

Eddie Brown, lead detective for the Riverville Police Department, answered the door to Abe's knock. His keen eyes studied his nephew, noting something different about him that day. He seemed more carefree, more relaxed than he had in years, Eddie thought, more than I've seen in him since that trouble all those years ago.

Abe took the cup of coffee his aunt Peg handed him. As she went to leave the kitchen, to let the two men talk together, he stopped her with a hand on her arm.

"Peg, can you stay? I need you to hear what I have to say as well. I'm going to need your help in what's coming up."

Peg and Eddie shared a glance. Peg then fixed her own cup of coffee and sat at the table with the two men. When Abe didn't speak, the married couple exchanged another glance. What was up with him, Eddie wondered?

"Abe? You said you needed to talk to us and that you needed our help. Care to explain?" Eddie's eyes searched his nephew's face.

Abe sighed, then spoke. "I'm really not sure where to begin." He stopped, trying to gather his thoughts. His whole world had just been turned upside down.

Eddie spoke. "Let's pray first, Abe. I sense that what you're about to share is going to shake up your world as well as ours."

Abe smiled. "That it will, Eddie. You don't know how much it will."

Sitting back in his chair when Eddie finished, Abe twisted his coffee cup in his hands. "I guess I need to go back to my last year in college. I met and fell in love with a wonderful woman. No one knew that we married about a month before school finished. She lived with a man who had married her aunt. My lady was the recipient of trust fund money from her parents. This man wanted it all. We married the day she turned 22, went to a lawyer and changed everything we could over to her married name and into both our names, visited the bank and moved all the trust fund monies to a new bank where no one could find it. The day after graduation, I dropped her off to pick up some stuff." Abe stopped, grief crossing his face. "I wish so much I had stayed with her that day. Driving back to pick her up, I was in a car accident and in hospital overnight. Dad never knew that, other than my car had been totaled.

"When I went back to get her, I was told that she wanted nothing more to do with me. I'm not sure what was going on there. I kept going back, every day for three months. Then, he had his men beat me up and drop me off 1,000 miles from there." Abe looked up at his uncle at that point.

Eddie nodded. "Your Dad and I came to get you. You were in hospital there for a while. You never would say what happened. Your Dad always wondered."

Abe nodded. "I know. I think I was in shock for a while, then just tucked it all away." He felt his aunt's hand on his. "Any way, I've always wondered what happened to her. I know you have all wondered why I never dated, never showed any interest in any lady. That's why, Eddie and Peg. She has my heart, and I can't give it to another."

"What happened today, Abe? Something has." Peg's voice was soft and full of concern.

Abe drew a deep breath. "Something did. Now that my guys are all settled with their ladies, I decided to try and find my lady. I thought Tracker's would be a good place to start. The thing is, I've only ever dealt with Jace there. I've never met Tracker, until today."

Eddie and Peg's eyes met, wonder in both of their faces. They had a good idea of what was coming but waited for Abe to speak.

"I heard Tracker's voice. When I approached her, she looked familiar. As I got closer, I realized it was her. It was my Emma, right here in my town." Abe's head went down on his folded arms and sobs shook his body. When he had control of his emotions, he continued, "That man had convinced Emma I had been killed in that car accident. He had paperwork to prove it that he showed her. I haven't talked her yet about what she went through. It was enough today to know that she's here and she still cares."

"Where do we come in, Abe?" Eddie's voice cut through the silence that had followed Abe's words.

"We both want this guy. We need to meet somewhere neutral to talk things through and make plans. Emma has a thick file, she says, that she's been compiling over the years. She wants to pass it on to you."

Peg spoke up. "Our home is open to you both. I'll go see her and make sure she's aware of that."

Abe nodded. "That's what I was hoping. It means a lot of time."

Eddie spoke. "We want this over for you, Abe, for you and your Emma. It's strange that you two have never met over the years. Let us open our home to you. It won't be strange if you come visit. We'll get your Emma here somehow."

The man stood watching Tracker's, waiting for her to leave. He could feel the authorities closing in on him. He knew she had another trust fund coming due. He would get that one, he thought. She had moved all the funds in the other one before he got to it. She would pay in more than one way for her treachery.

Emma turned in her office chair as Jace entered and sat in the chair in front of her desk, not saying anything, just watching her.

"He's the one, isn't he, Tracker? The one you've been grieving for all these years?"

She nodded, her eyes on her friend's face. "He is, Jace. Now, I'm not sure what name you should call me. You know my name's Emma, but I've been Tracker for so many years."

"Emma it is. You know Abe?"

She nodded and looked down at the wedding band on her hand. "We were married just before we finished college, Jace. When he dropped me off to pick up my things, my aunt's husband somehow managed to drug me. I was out for three days. When I woke, he had material proving Abe was dead." She pointed at a folder on her desk. "That's the material. I've never looked at it since he showed it to me. Maybe, I should have, but the grief was just so strong. One of his men helped me to get away. You found me on the streets about a month later, and took me home to your parents. I can't ever repay you, Jace, for your friendship and caring."

She watched as he shrugged. They had had this conversation many times over.

"So, I guess that picture of the eagle you were after and got was right after all. You told me if you ever got it you knew your life would straighten out." He stopped, looking down at the files on her desk. "I just don't get how you two never crossed paths."

"God, Jace. It had to be God. Timing was never right. Now it is." She leaned back in her chair. "I need to get on with my life. That now includes Abe." She turned the wedding band on her finger, watching the stones sparkle in the overhead light. "We've lost too many years."

"Okay." Jace sat forward. "So, what do we do?"

"We start with searching for this man, and any aliases he may have come up with. We set up a search for any widows or single women with trust funds that he came into contact with. Set the parameters for 12 years and within a thousand miles of my hometown. That will start." She stood and starting pacing, thinking better on her feet. "Abe's gone to talk with his uncle, to see if we can use their home as a meeting place for the next few weeks, just until we can get this all sorted out."

"His men will take it hard, not knowing what was going on with him."

Emma sighed, then nodded. "I just hope they don't blame me too much for what Abe's been through."

"They won't, Emma. I know they've been concerned about what's been going on with him that he won't talk about." Jace started to laugh, and Emma spun to stare at him. "I'm sorry, Emma. It's just that you two have been so close all these years. No one is going to believe that you didn't cross paths."

"We've crossed paths, Jace, just not close enough to recognize each other." She sighed again. "This is really going to put the pressure on what we're working through. Is Naomi up to coming in to work?"

Jace shook his head. "The doctor has her on bed rest for now. We're hoping to have her back on her feet in a week or so, but she won't be able to come into the office yet." He paused, then spoke again. "She's bored. If I can set up a computer or laptop for her to work from, she'd help." Jace's wife had been sick and was out of the office for the foreseeable future. "She'll never believe this, you do realize that?"

"No one will." She turned from her desk and headed for the door. "I'm off, Jace. I just can't work anymore today."

Jace stood and watched as she walked through the office to the back door and then left. He shook his head again. Who would have thought? He turned and grabbed the folders she had left for him, locked up the building and headed home. He just had to

spend time with his wife, and Naomi would
never believe him.

Chapter 3

Murphy watched as Abe headed for his personal SUV. It was strange, Abe going out every night. It was totally unlike him.

"What's up with, Abe?"

Murphy turned as Nathaniel spoke from beside him. "I have no idea. This is unlike him."

Nathaniel nodded. "I know. If it was anyone else, I would say he'd found a lady." Nathaniel shot a look at Murphy. "You've known him for years. Have you ever seen him date?"

Murphy had to think about that one. "Back in college, he was interested in a girl, but I don't know what happened to her. Once we were finished college, she just seemed to disappear."

"I wonder if that's what's been bothering him all along. We've all asked him, but he has never said."

"I know. I wish he would." Murphy turned to walk to his home. "I wonder what the meeting's about tomorrow. It's not like Abe to call a meeting on this short notice." Abe had spoken to each of his team members, letting them know he wanted to talk to them the next day.

Nathaniel shrugged. "Who knows? It's likely about a team coming in, or something new he wants us to try."

Abe paced his home the next day as he waited for the team members to gather. He had no idea how he was going to explain what he had to explain or how they would take it. The chiming of his phone caught his attention.

Pulling it out as he saw the men coming through his door, he looked down at it and smiled. Emma! She had known how he was feeling.

"God is with you, my love. Let Him speak. Luv you. Em."

The seven men found their coffee and then found seats in the living room, shooting glances at Abe and then one another. He wasn't acting like himself, Ian thought. What is going on?

Abe searched the faces of his friends, then nodded to himself. Lord, speak through me. Don't let this ruin our friendship or our working relationship. It could go bad so quickly.

"Thanks, guys, for giving me some time this afternoon. I know you're curious. First, let me say this isn't about work. This time, it's personal and this time it affects me." Abe paused, eyes on the floor as the men glanced at each other, frowns in place. "You have all asked me over time what I've been hiding, what's wrong, variations of that theme. I have never been able to talk about it." He stopped to run his hand through his dark blond hair, blue eyes shadowed.

"To explain, I have to go back to college. While there, I met a lady I fell in love with." Abe stopped, eyes on Murphy. Murphy's eyes narrowed as he thought about the girls in their group. Then his face cleared, and he nodded. He had a good idea of who Abe meant. "She came from a rich family, her parents dying when she was a young teenager and she was sent to live with an aunt. I'll come back to that.

"About a month before college ended, we married but kept it quiet." He didn't look up so missed the looks the men shared. "The day after graduation, I took her home to get her stuff and left. I had an accident on the way back. She was led to believe I was dead. I was led to believe by her aunt's husband that she didn't want anything to do with me. I tried every day for three months to find her at that house. I was finally beaten up and dumped miles away. Those of you who were hired by my father remember that. My lady had disappeared about a week after graduation. I had no idea where she was." Abe stopped speaking, overcome with emotion.

Ian spoke up. "That's incredible, Abe. I wish you had talked to us. We'd have found her for you." The other men agreed.

Abe looked up to find Murphy's thoughtful eyes on him. "You know her, Murphy. It's Emma."

Murphy nodded. "Emma. I always wondered if she was the one during college. You two certainly kept it quiet."

"We had to. She has trust funds left to her. She moved them the day we got married. She has another one coming up in a few weeks." He paused, shaking his head at what he had to say next.

"You will not believe it, but I can only say that God has been there, waiting for His own timing." He paused again, not sure how to finish.

"Spit it out, Abe. You always tell us that's the best way." Luke looked at him with a cheeky grin on his face.

Abe smiled at Luke's nonsense. "Then, I will. Emma is…." He paused again, still not sure how to proceed.

Murphy spoke up. "I think I can see where this is going. Emma is here in this town, right?"

Abe nodded. "How many times have I sent you guys to Tracker's?" He could see the dawning comprehension on their faces.

"And you've never been the one to go or even speak with her." Matt spoke up. "Tracker is Emma?"

Abe's eyes turned to Matt. He hesitated, then spoke. "She is, Matt. Now, you tell me, how do we live in the same town without meeting?"

Abe's confirmation left the men dumbfounded. They weren't quite sure how to react or even what to say.

Ian finally spoke. "I can see how it could happen, Abe. As you said, God was there. He had a purpose for this then, and a purpose now. When do we get to meet your lady? And where do we go from here?"

Abe smiled as he saw the acceptance on his friends' faces. He had worried for nothing. "If you're all around tomorrow, I'd like to have a dinner here, casual of course. Emma is unsure about meeting you and your wives."

"She's part of our family, Abe, has been without our knowing it. She's shouldn't worry." Joseph spoke for the group. "But as Ian has asked, where do we go from here with this?"

"Thanks, guys. As to where we go, Emma and Jace and his wife, Naomi, are pulling names and files every day, trying to find the aunt's husband. She's passing everything on to Eddie. Eddie and Peg have opened their home for us every night so we can talk things through and plan." Once again, Abe hesitated, knowing he had to speak, but unsure of how to phrase it.

Murphy had been watching him closely. "When do you renew your vows, Abe? I think that's what you're trying to say, isn't it?"

The men laughed at the look on Abe's face. "It is, Murphy. Only you would ask that at this point. We're planning on a week from Sunday. We've met with Greg Evans and are going forward with some plans. Those plans include going public with what happened all those years ago, and then working forward with how to find him."

"How do we help?" Micah spoke up. "If they need help with research I can free up some time, and so can Kat." His wife, Kat, researched family trees for both private and police personnel.

"I'll mention that to her, thanks, Micah."

The men finally left, talking quietly among themselves about the developments. Once thing they agreed on, they backed Abe fully. They would do what it would take to help him and Emma, just as he had with each of them. Their only question was, how would their wives react?

Adriel stared at Murphy. "What do you mean, Abe's married, and has been for years?"

"Just that, Elle. Just as I explained it." Murphy watched his wife. She had been at the same college as him, but they hadn't met until she ran into trouble in Riverville. Abe's team had been called in and they had fallen in love, marrying a few months previously.

"Emma?" Adriel thought over the women she had known there. "I don't remember her off hand, but Sue might." Sue was an officer on the Riverville police force and an old friend of them both.

"We're not prying into anything from college, Adriel. Abe needs our help now to sort through what's happened and to catch this guy."

"I still can't believe it. And to think it's Tracker." She spun around to face him. "That's it. I'm going to go find her tomorrow. If they're planning on renewing their vows in a week, she may need some help in the planning or whatever."

Murphy pulled his wife into a hug. "Thank you, my dear. Emma's worried about meeting all of us."

Emma looked up from her desk when Jace appeared at her door the next day. "Emma, there're some ladies here to see you. They've specifically asked for you."

She frowned, then looked down at her work. Sighing, she rose. "Did they say what they wanted?"

Jace shook his head, a smile on his face. "No, but I think you'll like them."

Emma walked slowly towards the front of the office. She disliked meeting new people, leaving that to Jace. She stopped as she counted eight, no, nine ladies, waiting for her. She walked forward to the reception area, her eyes scanning each of their faces.

"Emma, I'm Rebecca, Abe's sister." A blond woman stepped forward. "I have wanted to meet you for so many years. Welcome to our family." Rebecca reached to hug Emma.

Emma surprised, stood still for a moment, then reached to hug Rebecca back. "Thank you, Rebecca. Abe's spoken so much about you. I just wish it had been different. I've missed getting to know you." She drew back, arm still around her sister-in-law, and pointed at the other women. "You need to introduce me. I'm guessing these are the men's wives. But wait, we have an extra lady here."

Rebecca laughed. "This is Rachel, my sister-in-law, Gideon's sister. She's married to Ben Johnson's son, Timothy. When she found out what was going on, she refused to be left out."

Introductions made, Elizabeth, Nathaniel's wife spoke up. "I know we're doing dinner tonight, but we thought you might like some female support with your plans."

Emma's hands went to her face as she looked around. "It would be nice. I thought I would be doing it all on my own, with some support from Peg and Jace's wife, Naomi."

"Lead us to somewhere we can work, or is out here fine?"

"Here is fine. I'll lock the door."

Jace peeked into the area. "I'm off to work at home, Tracker. Sorry, Emma. Naomi has some stuff she needs to talk to me about."

Emma spun to stare at him, years of friendship letting her read his face. "Thank you, Jace. Yes, that's fine. Let me know what you two find out. Make sure Eddie and Abe get copies."

"Done. Nice to see you, ladies."

Emma watched as he walked away, then turned back to the ladies, who had seated themselves for the most part. "I have more chairs in the offices. Let's get them."

Once seated, Emma hesitated. "I hate to put you ladies at risk helping me. I've been told my aunt's husband is in the area and looking for me"

"He'll not know today that you are who you are. For all he knows, we've been meeting at each other's homes for months." Joseph's Leah spoke for the group.

Ian's Lydia nodded. "That's true. Now, Emma, tell us what you're planning and what we can do to help."

Immersed in the details, Emma looked up in surprise at the time. "You ladies need to get on your way. It'll soon be time for me to show up." She searched their faces. "By the way, who's cooking?"

Kat laughed. "Mac. He found out and offered to cater a cold meal for us. He's in his glory. He's so happy for you and Abe, Emma."

"And you'll never pay for another meal in his cafe again. He considers you family now." Matt's Sarah spoke up. "That's what he does."

Emma nodded, overwhelmed with the support. As she headed for her own home to change for the evening, she shuddered and looked around. Evil was stalking her, she thought, stalking her and drawing closer. She knew what Abe's team members had gone through. Lord, we need your protection now like we have never in the past. Please surround us now. Keep us each safe. Lead us in the way you would have us walk in the next few weeks and not months.

He had found her, he thought gleefully. He had finally found her. Who would have thought she would be hiding in plain sight? Soon, she would sign the paperwork and turn over the money she owed him. He turned and walked away to his vehicle. Now that he knew where she was, he'd wait until the right time.

Chapter 4

Emma stared into her closet, tears close to the surface. Her emotions were up and down these days. What did she wear? Her normal daily wear was faded T-shirts, worn jeans and sneakers. She had business clothes for when she needed to meet with clients or testify in court. Nothing that fit what she needed tonight. She sank back on her bed, a tear tracking down her cheek. She needed to shop, and she absolutely hated that.

She swiped at the tear as she rose to go answer the doorbell. She shot a glance at the clock. It was too early for Abe to be here.

She opened the door and then stood back for Abe to enter. He took one look at her face, dropped what he had in his hands and swept her into his arms.

"What's wrong, hon?"

She hugged him, then stepped back. "The age-old scourge of women. What do I wear? I have nothing suitable, didn't even think about it until now."

Abe bent to pick up the flowers he had dropped. "Here, these are for you." He handed her the yellow roses she loved. "Peg called me on the way in and sent a package for you. Somehow, she picked up on the fact that you don't like to shop and likely hadn't."

Peeking into the bag he handed her, she looked up, surprise on her face. "Why?"

"Why? Because you're family, Emma, that's why. Peg and Eddie look after their family." He watched the conflicting emotions crossing her face, knowing she hadn't had family for years. "She said she put in a few outfits, so that you could pick and choose what you want to wear."

She reached to hug him. "Thank you, Abe. I'll just be a few minutes now. The vases are above the fridge, if you could do the roses for me."

Abe watched as she almost ran to her bedroom, pulling the outfits out as she went.

Thank you, Peg, he thought. I never thought about what she would need for tonight. Then his heart raised in prayer, for his lady, for his team and their wives, and for the resolution of the trouble that had separated them and followed them for so many years.

Turning from the window he was watching through, he stopped, staring at Emma. Peg, you chose the colours and styles just right. Emma had chosen an embroidered denim skirt and matching blouse, her feet in sandals. He could tell she was still uncertain.

He reached for her, drew her into a hug, and then dropped a kiss on her mouth.

"Don't worry so much. The guys won't bite. Ian wanted to know why I hadn't said anything earlier. He would have found you for me, he said, as would the other guys."

She leaned her forehead on him. "That's good to know. Abe, I can feel Charlie around here. I think he's found out where I am."

Abe nodded, as he tucked her into his truck. "That's what Eddie's saying. He's been tracking his movements. He's in the area. This is where it will get dangerous, you know."

She nodded as her eyes searched the area. "I guess I never thought farther than next week about what we do. You have, I know."

Abe nodded as he headed back to his home. "I have. I've been talking with Eddie. Now that we have the information you've provided today, he'll be talking with both Caleb and Frankie." Caleb Logan was the Riverville Police Chief and Frankie Brennan, a former street cop turned detective. Both men, around Abe's age, were close friends.

Emma sat back in her deck chair in the early evening, watching the activity around her. She was tired, but the acceptance she had found had eased the burdens she carried. She looked up as Murphy dropped into a chair beside her, tilting her head to watch his face. He's not sure how to proceed, is he, Lord? He wants to ask questions and is trying to find the words.

"Spit it out, Murphy. We were friends in college, although not close ones." Emma smiled at the look on his face.

"That we were, Emma." Murphy watched the emotions flickering on her face, and saw the fatigue weighing there. "I never knew you two were that close. I don't think any of us did."

She shook her head. "We kept it as quiet as we could. We didn't want word getting back to Charlie, although somehow he found out." She leaned her head back and stared at the darkening sky, the moon just making its presence known. "Maybe if we had been more open, we wouldn't have lost all those years."

"Or maybe both of you would be dead." Her eyes shot to him at that. "I remember meeting him once. He has a cruel, sadistic personality. He would have made you suffer."

"And he's trying that now. He's in the area."

Murphy looked towards where Abe stood talking with Gideon and Ian. "I'm sure he is. I'm also sure he knows where you are living." His eyes came back to Emma. "Tell me, Emma, what can we do to help you?"

She shook her head. "I'm not even sure. Jace and Naomi are pulling more and more material on him. He's known as the black widower in police circles. No one has been able to catch him."

Murphy nodded and looked up as Adriel sat on the arm of his chair. "We'll do what we can to keep you two safe."

Later, driving Emma back home, Abe reached for her hand. "It wasn't so bad, was it?"

Emma laughed. "I made it out to be worse in my head than it was. You have a great team there, Abe, and their ladies are so special.”

“We think they are.” He paused as he went to turn into her driveway. “Did you leave any lights on in your office or your house?”

She shook her head. “Just the outside light on the house.”

Abe shot a look around him, then backed into an abandoned driveway. “There are low lights on in both buildings.” He pulled out his phone and called for a patrol car. “We’ll wait here. You said earlier you thought he had been around?”

She nodded. “I know he has been. I get these feelings and they’re usually bang on.”

Frankie walked towards them an hour later, stopping to lean on the SUV door and stare in at them.

“Abe. Tracker. I wasn’t aware you two knew each other.”

Emma started to giggle, drawing a frown from Frankie. “I’m sorry. My name is actually Emma, Frankie.”

“Emma, is it?” He turned probing eyes to Abe. “That doesn’t explain why you’re here, Abe.”

Abe took a look at Emma, then sighed. "It's a long story, Frankie, one that will be coming out soon."

"I like long stories. Emma, your house has been cleared. It doesn't look like anything has been disturbed, but we'd like you to go through it for us."

Emma nodded, then waited for Abe to come around and open her door. Hand tight in his, she walked towards her home, Frankie's speculative eyes on them.

She turned finally. "I don't see that anything has been disturbed, Frankie. Any of my important documents and anything I am working on are always locked in my safe." She turned to the kitchen. "Let me put on coffee for you two. I can see it's going to be a long night."

Abe watched as she paused in the kitchen doorway, then walked towards her. "What's wrong, Emma?"

"Your roses. They're gone. We left them on the kitchen counter earlier."

Abe stilled. "You're right. What would someone want with the roses?"

"Charlie. It has to be him. I'll get them back in a few days, dead. But how did he get in?"

"Care to explain who Charlie is?"

Abe and Emma had forgotten Frankie for a minute. Emma sighed, went to start the coffee, then turned to Frankie. "Have a seat at the table, Frankie. This is going to take a while and you'll not be believing what we say."

Frankie sat back, shaking his head in disbelief. "Really? All that? And you never said a word, Abe."

Abe shook his head. "It hurt too much, I guess. No one has guessed, other that Micah's Kat. She told me one day that whoever I gave my heart to still loved me." He reached for Emma's hand.

Emma made a mental note to find Kat in the next few days.

"So, was it him then, Frankie?" Emma's quiet question caught at Frankie's heart.

"I don't know, Tracker, I'm sorry, Emma. It might have been. We'll pull your video surveillance and logs, but if it's him, he may have hired someone to break in."

"Not his style. He would do it himself just to threaten and try and put fear into me."

Frankie rose. "You say you've given Eddie data?"

She nodded. "He said he'd be speaking with you and Caleb now."

Frankie shared a look with Abe. "I don't need to tell you two to be very careful." He walked towards the door, his next sentence floating behind him. "And, Abe, let's not have an adventure like your people have had."

"Or like you, Frankie?" Abe's reminder stopped Frankie in his tracks and caused him to turn around.

"Or like me. We've had enough of those kind of adventures."

"Sorry, Frankie, but somehow I don't think we're done yet. We still have a few friends to work through."

Frankie shook his finger at Abe. "No. Not going there, Abe. I'll be in touch, Emma, when I find out what the crime scene team found."

Abe turned to Emma after Frankie had closed the door. "Are you okay to stay here?"

She shrugged. "I should be. He won't be back tonight. It's not his style."

Abe studied her face. "I can take you to Peg, or back to my place."

She shook her head. "No, I'll be fine, Abe. I have a weapon. I'm not afraid to use it if he comes back."

"If you're sure?"

"I am. Go, you have things you need to be doing in the morning."

He reached to drop a kiss on her face, then turned. He stopped as if to say something, then continued to walk through the door and back to his vehicle. How do I walk away tonight, Lord, and every night for the next few days? Keep her safe. Put a hedge of protection around her, please, dear Lord. I can't lose her now I've found her again.

Chapter 5

Abe leant his arms on his knee as he leaned forward to speak with his cousin, Doug Foster, sitting beside Emma in the last pew of their church. His eyes stared into the distance as he listened to what Doug was asking, then turned to study Emma. She nodded.

"That would be fine, Doug. We'll be away next week, but any time the next week should be fine." He looked past Doug as his wife, Deidre, turned back to them.

At the end of the service while the last song was being sung, Abe stepped from the pew, shrugging his suit coat into place and buttoning it as he waited for Emma to walk before him to the back of the church. He reached for her hand, exchanged a glance with her, then walked into the hallway towards the room where Emma would change. She hadn't said what she was changing into, only that she needed a room. Darcy followed them, as did Rebecca, slipping past them into the room.

Abe stared down at Emma's face, then touched it without a word, before turning and walking towards the pastor's office. Greg Evans would come find them when it was time.

Greg approached the pulpit and raised his hand. The end of service movement stopped as the congregation watched him.

"Before you go, I have something I need to say and a statement to read from the board. Before I do that, I just want to say that what is upcoming brings a lot of joy to many people who know the two involved.

"You all know Abe Finlay, have since he was a child. Some of you know what he went through a few years ago. Some of you don't. That's his story to share.

"What I am about to say is hard to do. Abe married his college sweetheart a month before they graduated. The day after they graduated, they were separated by a cruel greedy man. Abe thought his wife no longer wanted to see him, his wife thought he had been killed in a staged car accident.

"A few weeks ago, Abe walked into a business here in Riverville and found his wife, after ten years. God led him there that day. Who is his wife? We know her as Tracker. Her name is Emma.

"Abe and Emma have met on numerous occasions with me over the last two weeks. Not needing to, they have also met with our church leadership.

"Now this is the statement I have been asked to read by the leadership. My prayer is that you will respect Abe and Emma's wishes and the wishes of your leadership." Greg paused for a moment, to send a quick prayer to heaven.

"As your church leadership, we have met with Abe Finlay and Emma Donovan Finlay. The leadership does not need to approve of their marriage. God has already done that. Through circumstances beyond their control, they have led separate lives for ten years. God has brought them back together and their wish is to continue their marriage as they had planned.

"Your church leadership will brook no gossip regarding these two. Anyone who chooses to gossip will be dealt with in a loving, God-managed way. Please join us in wishing Abe and his lady Emma a long God-blessed marriage."

Greg folded the paper he had been reading from. "In a short while, Abe and Emma will be renewing their marriage vows right here, today. They have opened it up to whoever wants to stay. Thank you."

Greg turned and walked from the dais, leaving stunned silence in his wake. Eddie and Peg stood and moved away from the sanctuary, followed by Abe's friends and team members.

Abe stood beside Doug, waiting for Emma to come towards him, Doug's wife, Darcy, serving as her matron of honour. He turned, catching his breath at her beauty. She hadn't told him what she was wearing. The ivory wedding dress and veil brought out the beauty he had always seen.

Eyes and hands steady, they faced each other, saying the vows they had said so many years ago and lived true to.

Greg watched the two, then nodded. God was in this, he thought. Please, Lord, I know what they're planning. Please, please, keep them safe and unharmed.

Abe turned to Emma as she stood watching his friends mingle and laugh with one another.

"You've become part of a large group, you know, my love."

"I see that. I've never been part of a group like this. Don't worry if there are times I need to run and hide."

"Just so long as I can go with you." He looked down at her again. "One day, you'll need to take me to where you fly with the eagles."

She smiled. "I would love that."

Murphy watched the two walk from the church, then turned as Ian approached.

"This is where it's going to be difficult, you know, Murphy."

"I know, Ian. I can feel the evil approaching, just like it did with each of us. Abe's not going to be wanting to let go of the planning."

Ian nodded. "I suggest that as a team, we get together this week and make some plans of our own. I have a gut feeling we're going to need them."

Caleb's wife, Hannah, turned to him as he drove away from the church. "Did you have any idea, Caleb?"

He shook his head. "None whatsoever. I always wondered, when I had occasion to speak with her, what brought the sadness into her eyes and face."

Hannah nodded. "I fear for them, Caleb. I think they've just begun their fight."

Caleb's eyes turned to his wife, then back to the road. "We already know who is after her."

"You have a name and a picture. What you don't have is who he's hired."

Chapter 6

Emma was on a search. She had moved most of her things to Abe's home, but she couldn't find her laptop. She knew she had brought it with her. Stopping in the home office, she spun, trying to remember where it was. Then, she nodded. It was in the business office. She had left it there the night before.

She headed across the area towards the office, stopping in her tracks as the sense of evil almost overwhelmed her. She turned to study the hills and rocks around her, then turned towards where she knew the lake was. Where is he, Lord? He's around here somewhere.

Luke watched her, then turned his own eyes to the area around them. Their compound had been breached from there before, and some of the team had been assaulted up there. There had been evidence found over the months that someone was up there watching them, in particular, Abe. He approached Emma, startling her when he spoke.

"You feel it, don't you, Emma?"

She spun, hand going to her chest. "I do, Luke. It's the same feeling I had at my own place."

"You're heading for the office?" Luke turned to walk with her.

"I am. I think I left my laptop there, and I need to do some research for a client."

Luke held the door for her. There was a team in for training in security, and Abe was in the training building. She walked towards his desk, then stopped to scan the room.

"Who set up this room?"

Her question caught Luke unawares. "Abe and Murphy did. They changed it after Abe took over the business when his Dad died."

She nodded. "They've done well. Everything you could need is right here."

Luke's eyes watched her face. There was something going on here, Lord, not related to this room.

Emma finally turned to Luke. "Tell me, what is your actual task with the team?"

"Armaments, weapons, knowledge of them. I'm the one who finds those and disarms them if needed when we're out on a security task. I also do training in that with our teams, not defusing them, but what to look for."

Emma nodded, a thoughtful look on her face. "Somehow, Luke, I have a feeling we'll need your expertise in the near future."

"You think you will?" Luke was taken aback at her words.

She nodded. "From what Jace, Naomi and I have dug up about Charlie, I'm sure we'll need the expertise of every one of you at some point, unless God intervenes before that."

She reached for her laptop, then turned to the man standing staring at her. "Don't worry, Luke. Abe and I have talked over all the possibilities we could and likely will face. He'll be talking with you all." She walked away, leaving him staring at her, shaking her head.

Now what, Lord? Is Abe going to have to go through what each of us did?

Abe stood leaning against the kitchen counter as he listened to Emma on the phone with Jace. His team had gathered as well as he wanted to talk with them.

"Jace, I think we need to increase the parameters. I'm not getting what I want from our search."

"How far back should we go?"

"I would say twenty, twenty-five years, increase the distance to three thousand miles." She stared into the distance, lost in thought. The men watched with interest at the conflicting emotions flickering across her face. "I think we also need to increase the age parameter."

"Increase it? We're already running 40 to 55 in years."

"I know. But I don't think that's enough. Go from 30 to 60. Include anyone who has a trust fund or access to one. I would also add a parameter of someone who died within two years of meeting and/or marrying him. Also look for transfer of large sums of money out of the country for those women."

"Are you serious, Emma? That's not your veggies talking, is it?

Emma laughed at that. "No, Jace, I've given up the suckers and chocolate, at least for now. So, you can stop bugging me about my veggies." Matt and Nathaniel snickered at that point, remembering her definition of a veggie, and she glared at them. "No, I have a feeling that he's responsible for multiple deaths. I've spoken with the police chief and chief coroner in my hometown. Given what I've found, they're arranging for a warrant to disinter Auntie Em for an autopsy. One wasn't done when she died."

The men standing around her exchanged glances, then looked at Abe. Abe's eyes were on his wife, a concerned look on his face.

"You think he's responsible?"

"Given what he did to Abe and me, I'm sure he is. She was never sick, had no chronic diseases. So, how did she die? My feeling is that he paid off someone to cover it up. Catch up with me later, Jace." She clicked her phone, eyes on her hands.

Abe's hands on her shoulders startled her, and she spun to face him.

"Do you really think that, Emma?" Abe's voice had a note of caring and concern.

"I do, Abe. It's just never sat right, how she died so quickly."

Micah spoke up. "That's an interesting search you're doing."

Emma looked up, startled that he had picked up on that. "That's what we do, Micah. Jace has written a program that allows us to search like that. It's not common knowledge, though."

"Kat would love to hear about it, if you ever decide to share. She had one something like that."

"I know she did. I've used it on occasion." Emma's eyes searched each man standing in the kitchen. "So, now that you're all here, is there a reason?"

Abe wrapped her in his arms from behind her. "There is. We need to discuss how we go about trying to catch this Charlie, and how to keep you safe as well."

Emma snorted in a very unladylike manner. "Include yourself in that, Abe. He's not going to let you get away from him either. You're dangerous to his freedom."

Abe nodded, as he thought about that. "That's true enough. But you're the one he'll go after."

"Not necessarily, Abe." Nathaniel spoke up. "With you two going public with your marriage, he knows you'll be looking for him. He's also responsible for what happened to you. If he can use you to get to Emma, then he will.”

Abe stared down at his wife, until she broke away from him and started pacing the hallway. His eyes followed her, then searched the faces of each of the men standing or sitting in the kitchen. His gaze lingered on Murphy.

“She never used to pace, did she, Abe?” Murphy was concerned at this change in Emma.

“No, she didn’t. When I asked her, she says she thinks better when she’s moving.”

“Her thought processes were always scary in class. I think the professors were afraid of her.”

Abe laughed. “That they were. Okay, guys, now what? You’ve told me I’m a target. I can tell you I don’t like that a bit.”

The seven men started laughing, and Abe shot them a questioning look.

“Sorry, Abe, you sounded just like each one of us at some point.” Matt shook his head.

Abe sighed, then laughed with them. “I guess I do. I don’t like it, though.”

"All those messages we've received over the past few months, directed at you?" Joseph looked around at the group, then leaned back to watch Emma. "Are they from him?"

Emma appeared at Joseph's side. "Letters? I didn't know about those, Abe." She glared at him. "How can I figure out what he's up to if you don't give me all the information I need?"

"Draw in the claws, Emma. We hadn't got to that point in the discussion. Yes, each one of these men received a note, directed at me, but threatening them as well. At least two have experienced his actions, the last one being Micah. I have a folder of them I'll get to you."

Joseph laid his hand on her arm. "We're trying to come up with everything we have or every contact we have had with him for you and Jace. Eddie and Frankie are working on that as well. But what we need to do now is make sure both you and Abe are safe. Abe is usually with one of us. What do we do about you?"

She stared at Abe, eyes not wavering. "I'm not hiding any longer. If he was standing out in the yard right now, I'd be in his face. I refuse to let him have any more control over me." She turned and almost ran from the house, letting the door close softly behind her.

They stared after her. Abe dropped his head in frustration. *Lord, what do I do? How do I do this? How do we keep her safe?*

The door opened again, and he saw Frankie standing here looking behind him. He moved towards him.

Frankie turned at his footsteps. "What's with your wife, Abe? She almost ran me down."

"Joseph just informed her we were trying to come up with a plan to keep her safe, and she's not having any part of it."

"I didn't think she would. Can you go find her? She needs to hear what I have to say."

Chapter 7

Emma sat, staring with an impassive look on her face and an inscrutable look in her eyes at Frankie. He stared back at her. The men surrounding them wondered who would blink first. They decided it would be Frankie.

Frankie spoke, his eyes still on Emma. "Abe, do you have that material you were gathering up for me?"

Abe reached behind him to the counter and slid it across the table. "Here is it. I think we've covered just about every time there was an incident. Although there may have been some we didn't know or think were related to him."

Frankie nodded. "I suspect there are some. Now, Emma, talk to me. Tell me about your aunt's husband."

Emma shook her head. "I've done that so many times for you already, Frankie. I can think of nothing to add."

Frankie finally broke eye contact with her and looked down at the folder on the table. "Are you sure?"

Emma rose. "I am sure. One thing I will not tolerate, Frankie, now or at any time, is someone questioning whether I am being truthful or frank with him. Abe has all that I can remember in that folder as well. If you have new questions, come find me." She turned to Abe. "I'm off. I need to go find Jace."

Abe watched as she once more walked away from him, then turned to Frankie, who was staring after her.

"Did she really just do that?" Frankie turned back to Abe, furious with Emma.

"Back off, Frankie. She knows the risks, she knows him better than anyone else at this time. If he wanted to get to her, he would." Abe stopped, thinking through his and Emma's many discussions. "She has shares in a company coming up for distribution in a couple of weeks. There is also her aunt's trust fund coming up to be distributed to her at the same time. She has already taken steps to have those funds and shares transferred from her to a new company that will distribute those funds as needed to the charities she's chosen. As soon as midnight the night they come to her, they're transferred. She won't go back on that for anyone."

Ian looked up at that. As the paralegal for the team, he was interested in how she had set that up. "It's irrevocable, is it, Abe?"

Abe nodded. "I was with her two weeks ago when she spoke with her lawyer. She is adamant that she doesn't want the money."

Frankie nodded as he listened to Abe's words. "So, he would get nothing now or then." When Abe shook his head, he spoke, "Then, it's revenge and retaliation, plain and simple." He looked around at the team, reading their grim looks correctly. "I don't need to tell you to be careful. How are you dealing with Emma's safety?" He looked startled as the men all laughed.

"We've been trying to deal with that, Frankie." Murphy shook his head. "That's why she almost ran you down."

"What do Caleb and Eddie say?" Abe's quiet question broke through the moment.

"About what you think they would say. Caleb is not happy that another one of you is a target. He wants this over yesterday."

"I'm sure he does. So, do I. The man stole enough from me." Abe looked up as the door opened again, and Emma appeared.

Emma was furious. How did Charlie get through security to her car?

"Here, Frankie. He left this in my car. You tell me, how did he get through all this security to do so?" Emma thrust an envelope at him.

"You're sure it's from him."

She nodded. "I know his handwriting. I haven't seen it in over ten years, but it's him." Her words were biting. "So, Abe, tell me. How did he do it?"

Abe shot a look at Joseph, who nodded and left with Ian. "It's been done before, Emma. They come down through the rocks. We can't put security up there. We talked about that."

Ian walked back into the kitchen, a strange look on his face. "Emma, I have a gentleman here to speak with you."

She turned, looking past him. Then a look Abe couldn't describe flickered across her face as she moved towards the living room. He followed, staring at the tall, thin gentlemen dressed in a dark suit, with graying hair, who was smiling at his wife.

"Antonio? Tony? Why are you here?"

Tony, as she had called him, reached for her hands, then kissed her on both cheeks. "Tracker, or should I say Emma? I heard through the grapevine that you were here and facing some difficulties of your own."

"I am, Tony, but your kind of help can't fix it."

He bowed his head. "I no longer do that kind of help." He pointed a finger at her. "Your help changed my family. My wife and daughters - I cannot thank you for what you did. I have my son back. Through you, we have learned what life is all about."

Emma's eyes shone with unshed tears. "Oh, Tony, you did it? You believed?"

At his nod, she continued, "But…"

His finger on her lips, he stopped her. "I worked with the authorities. I am no longer in that business. I did a couple of years and at present am on house arrest." He lifted a pant leg to show the tracking bracelet. "I received special permission to come see an old friend and offer my help." His eyes went behind her to Abe. "But, somehow, I don't think you'll need it."

Emma reached for Abe's hand. "Abe, this is Tony, I guess you would say an old friend? Tony, this is the man you asked me about years ago. This is my husband."

Tony studied the two of them. "Abe Finlay? Your father was Peter?" At his nod, he continued, "Your father did me a service many years ago, that you won't find on the books. I said then I would help either one of his children when the time came. That time is now." He turned to Emma. "You too, my dear lady. You don't know what you have done to my family, but it is all for the better. I hear that you are after Charlie. So are former friends of mine. I have spoken with them. They will grant you one month, then they are going after him." Tony watched her face, then nodded. "You know where to find me if you need me." He turned and walked from the house.

Frankie had watched with interest during Emma's conversation. He turned as he heard movement from Abe's team. Each man had stood where he could watch Emma and Abe.

"Wasn't that...?" Matt's voice died away, not quite sure of what he had witnessed.

Emma turned around to stare at the men. "That was my friend, Tony. I have picked up friends in many different walks of life. I can't and won't explain how I know him, other than what you heard." She looked at Frankie. "We have one month. Can we do it?"

He shrugged. "It's a tight timeline but let's get to work. I suggest that we convene at the department and I'll pull in whoever I need."

Emma shook her head. "You work with what you have. I have other ideas that I want to work through."

He looked down at the envelope in his hand. "I'll get this to our crime team, but I'm not confident we'll find anything." He walked away with that.

Abe looked around at the team members remaining. There was no question now that they would work their magic as best they could, keep both Emma and Abe safe, and search for the man responsible.

Chapter 8

Abe turned as he heard his name called. Caleb was walking towards him, both of them headed for Mac's, a local cafe.

"Caleb."

"Abe. This is good timing. I've been wanting to touch base with you." The men slid into a booth, and Mac waved at them, heading for the kitchen to put in their orders. "Where does Emma and Jace stand with their investigation?"

Abe shook his head. "She hasn't said much in the last two days since Frankie was out. She did say it takes a few days to run a search the size she's running."

"I still don't get how she knows what to search for or the time frame."

"It's how her mind works. She always scared the professors." Abe looked up as Mac set their food in front of them. "Thanks, Mac."

"You're welcome, Abe. SuEllen wants you and Emma to come over for a meal soon."

"We'll do that. Have her call Emma."

"Emma still as unsure about how big a family she's now a part of, Abe?"

Abe nodded. "She is. She only had her aunt when her parents were killed overseas. She has never liked Charlie. She said she always felt a presence of evil around him."

Caleb nodded. "You have done a lot of leg work for us already, Abe, between your team and Emma and Jace. We're verifying it. He's a nasty piece of work."

"That he is." Abe stopped, then shook his head, smiling. "I told the guys I didn't like being a target. They just laughed at me."

Caleb started laughing at that. "I guess they would. You know now what they felt like. What steps are you taking now?"

"Emma would like to do a news interview, hoping to draw him out. I'm trying to talk her out of that right at the moment."

"I can imagine how hard that would be." Caleb stopped speaking, not sure how to broach the subject he knew he needed to.

"Frankie said Emma had an interesting visitor when he was there."

"Tony Marchionda. I wouldn't have thought she knew him. I guess she helped him out years ago." He sat back, eyes on Caleb's face. "He said my Dad did as well."

"That's an interesting comment for him to make. You had no idea?"

Abe shook his head. "He said we'd never find evidence of it, but he promised to help either Emma or I if we ever needed it. I'm not sure what he's up to, though"

"I would gather he's put men in town to watch out for you two. A scary thought, that."

"It is. Listen, I need to run. I have a meeting with the team about a security detail we've been asked to do next week. I'm really not sure about it though."

"After what happened with Kat, all I can say is be very careful. Do your research. Have Emma search them out for you." Caleb grinned at the look Abe sent him.

"I'm sure she already has. She's scary that way."

"I thought only Frankie's wife, Deirdre, was scary."

Abe shook his head again. "Emma has her beat hands down. She even scared our professors at college."

Emma turned as Abe walked into the home office and reached to kiss her. "This is nice. What time's your meeting?"

"In about an hour. Mac said SuEllen wants to have us in for a meal."

Emma nodded, trying to place who she was.

"That's Mac's wife, from the cafe. He's related to us."

Emma's face cleared. "I need a people map to keep track of everyone, you know. There are just so many people."

Abe perched on the corner of the desk. "Can't keep people straight, but can find anyone you need to?" He had a spark of mischief in his eyes.

She smacked his leg. "Behave, Abe. What else did you find out in town?"

"Just that Caleb thinks you're scarier that Frankie's wife, Deidre."

She looked at him in astonishment as he laughed. "That's not a nice thing to say."

"It is if you know the story of how Frankie and Deirdre met and fell in love. They've asked us in for a meal one night next week. I said you'd call Deirdre."

She nodded, lost in thought. "Abe, what if we don't find Charlie?"

"Then, you heard Tony. His friends will take care of him."

"I know, but it's not justice for us." She sighed. "There I go again, trying to do God's work for him. All we can do, I guess, is pray for His protection to surround us."

"That we can do. Listen, I have to run. I've got some information to dig up before our team meeting.

"Abe, can you let me know the name of who it is? I don't have a good feeling about it."

"Sure." He reached for a pad of paper and a pen. "You're not the only one. My guys are running scared after what happened the last time we were out of town."

She took the paper from him, then froze. "Abe, you can't go. I know this name. He's a contract killer."

"You're sure?"

She nodded and turned to her computer, pulling up a secure program and then typing in the name. She pointed at the information she brought up.

Abe read it, then kissed his wife. "Thank you, sweetheart. This solves whether we're away next week."

"So, what will you do instead?"

Abe studied her, not having been asked that question before. "We do our own training, keeping our skills sharp. We have a team of six coming in the following week." He stopped as he saw the look on her face. "Let me guess, you want to check out this team as well?"

"I do. Knowing Charlie, he could bring in someone to our home, and we'd never know."

He sat back, staring into the distance. That thought was scary. He directed his eyes back to Emma and found her staring at him. "You're right, Emma. Until this is over, Murphy or I will give you the names of teams applying for training, and you can work your magic for us."

"Go. Let your team know you're not travelling next week." She turned back to what she had been working on.

Abe stood and walked to the door, his face turning back to watch his wife. Then he shook his head and walked out to the business office.

The watcher stood in the rocks once again. It was becoming a habit with him, to stand there and watch Abe and his team. Now, he had Emma to watch as well. They were being too careful, he thought. How could he get to the two he wanted, if they were never on their own? He turned and walked away, back to his vehicle, deep in thought. Somehow, he would separate them from those other men, and he would have them in his control.

Chapter 9

Abe turned to Emma as they headed home after dinner with Mac and SuEllen. "You had a good time tonight?"

"I did. They're such a sweet couple. I've heard of all the good they've done over the years in town. Kat mentioned how good they were to her when she moved to town"

Abe nodded, as he slowed to make a turn. "They were. He's always been like that."

Emma felt something shift in the vehicle. "Abe, what was that?"

"I don't know, but I think the brakes are gone. Make sure your seatbelt is tight. This is not a nice section of the road."

Emma's fingers whitened as she gripped both her seatbelt and her door handle. She had confidence in Abe's ability to handle the vehicle, but not in the road they were travelling.

Abe's fingers tightened on the wheel. The vehicle was picking up speed, no matter how low he shifted gears. He shot a quick glance at Emma. She seems calm, he thought. Then, his attention was drawn to a slow-moving vehicle ahead of them. He had no choice, he had to go around it.

Emma screamed as the SUV hit the dirt on the opposite of the road and then left the road. Abe struggled to keep it upright, but he couldn't. He felt the vehicle as it rolled, then blackness overcame him.

Matt slammed on the brakes and pulled to the side of the road. He turned to Sarah. "Call 911. I think that's Abe's vehicle. I'm going to check." He scanned the area around them. The other vehicle he had seen was gone. That's strange, he thought.

Matt slid down the slight incline and up to the vehicle. His heart in his mouth, he reached for the driver's door. Somehow, the SUV had ended up on its wheels. He wasn't able to open that door, so he headed for the other side. This time, he was able to pry the door open. Emma slumped in the seat, and he reached for her wrist. She was alive. Reaching across her, he felt for Abe and felt his pulse strong and steady. He breathed a sigh of relief, then turned as he heard footsteps behind him. Sarah stood there, phone in hand.

"They're asking for a status on the injured, Matt, if you know."

He reached for her phone. "They're alive, Sarah. I just don't know how hurt they are."

She nodded, then looked around, shivering.

"What wrong, Sarah?" Matt asked as he handed her back her phone. He had put in a call to Murphy when he had finished with the dispatch.

"I feel evil, Matt, just like with us. Only it's a stronger, deeper feeling."

Matt scanned the area. "I know. Both Abe and Emma have mentioned it." He turned as he heard movement in the car.

Emma turned, trying to escape the bounds holding her. She heard a familiar voice, but couldn't place him. Darkness dropped down on her again.

The paramedics and firefighters worked to stabilize and then remove the two. Frankie stood on the shoulder, staring at the vehicle, then moved to stand beside Matt.

"How'd you get here?"

"We were in town and headed home when we saw the SUV suddenly swerve to the left and then leave the road. We didn't know it was Abe at first." Matt turned to look around the area. "The thing of it is, Frankie, there was another vehicle here. It was in front of Abe's and moving very slowly." He turned back to look at Abe's vehicle. "I think you need to check his brakes. He didn't seem to be able to slow down."

Frankie stared at him. "His brakes? Are you saying they failed?"

"Not on their own." Sarah stood beside Matt. "At least, I don't think so. Abe seemed to be trying to slow the vehicle down. He just might have done it except for that other vehicle, and before you ask, we didn't get a good look at it."

Frankie nodded. "I'll have it towed to our garage and have our techs go over it. Any word on how they are?"

Matt shook his head. "Not yet. I'm heading back in to the hospital, and Murphy's on his way. I daresay Rebecca and Gideon will be there too."

"Let me know how they are. I'll also need to get a report from you, if you haven't given it yet."

"We have, Frankie, to the responding officers."

Adriel's hand in his, Murphy strode through the Emergency Room doors, eyes searching for his friends. He knew some of them were on their way, some already here. He saw Rebecca and Gideon and made his way to them.

"Rebecca, any word yet?"

Rebecca looked up, tears streaking her cheeks. "Not yet, Murphy. They're still evaluating them."

Adriel reached to hug Rebecca, then sat beside her. "God has them in His hands, Rebecca. We need to remember that."

She nodded. "I know but it's hard to trust at a time like this."

Gideon wrapped his arm around his wife's shoulders. "He'll be okay, Rebel."

Murphy turned as he heard his name called. Jace was walking towards him.

"Have you heard anything yet, Murphy?"

"No. I just got here. How'd you find out?"

"I'm next after Abe as her medical power of attorney. They called me in, just in case."

Murphy's eyes slid shut. "Have they told you anything yet?"

"No, other than she was stable."

Jace turned as he heard his name called and walked towards the nurse. He followed her back to the exam room area, stepping through the door she indicated. He studied the face of his friend lying there, bruised with a few scrapes. Thank you, Lord, she's alive.

Emma stirred, her eyes opening as she stared around, then sliding closed as she realized where she was.

"Emma?"

She opened her eyes to see Jace standing there, concern on his face. "Jace." She had to clear her throat to get his name out. "What are you doing here?"

"I got a call a friend was hurt and needed me. How you feeling?"

"Like I've been run over by a Mack SUV." She turned her head, panic starting to set it. "Abe? Where's Abe?"

"He's in the next room. I haven't been told how he is."

"Help me up, Jace."

He shook his head. "They want you to stay here."

She sat up, waited for the room to stop spinning, then swung her legs off the side of the stretcher. "If you don't help me, I'll go myself."

Jace held up his hands in surrender, then reached to help her down. A nurse passing by stopped and shook her head.

"You need to be lying down, Mrs. Finlay."

"No. What I need is to see my husband. Which room, or do I have to search each one?"

The nurse pointed to the one beside where she had been. "In there. I'll let the doctor know where you are."

Emma drew a deep breath, then shoving Jace aside, pushed the door open and moved forward to stand beside Abe. He was still unconscious, battered, bruised. She touched his face, then looked for a chair to sit in. Jace, anticipating her need, set one beside her, then walked away, back to the waiting room. He found Murphy, had a few words with him and then left. Emma didn't need him, he knew.

Murphy turned to find eyes on him. He approached the team members. "Emma's up and on her feet. She's bruised and sore. Jace didn't hear of any serious injuries."

"What about Abe?" Matt had been there since Abe was brought in but hadn't heard anything.

"I haven't heard anything yet. If I don't hear in the next few minutes, I'll go find the doctor." He turned as he heard his name called and walked forward to meet the physician. It was John Thompson, a friend from church.

"I hear you're Abe's power of attorney after Emma?"

Murphy blinked, having forgotten that. "I guess I am. How is he, John?"

"God's hand was on the two of them tonight, Murphy. Come, I'll take you back. Emma's already found him." John pushed the door open for Murphy to enter the cubicle. "He's got bruised ribs, other bruising and a few cuts. He's been awake."

"That's good news, John. Are you keeping them overnight?"

"Seeing as it's so late, I think so. They'll not likely be here long enough to go to a room. Emma's already threatening to go find you guys to help her take Abe home." John looked at Emma, who had laid her head down on the pillow near Abe and slept.

"I can see her doing just that, John. You'll have to watch her. What time do you want us here in the morning to pick them up?"

"I'll do rounds about 6 a.m. before I sign off to the morning physician. Any time after that should be fine."

Emma stirred as she heard the early morning bustle of the department. She raised up and stretched, stiff from the accident and stiff from the night spent sleeping like she had. Her hand went to Abe's face.

Abe stirred, feeling Emma's hand on his face. His eyes opened, and he looked around, everything blurry. He kept blinking until everything cleared. He turned, finding Emma very close to him.

"Hi." Her eyes were concerned as she searched his face.

"Hi, sweetheart. Where are we?"

"You don't remember?" When Abe shook his head, she frowned. "We had a car accident last night on the way home from dinner."

Abe searched his memory, but couldn't remember it at all. "Did I total another car?"

She smiled. "You did. Except this time I was with you. Frankie wants to talk with you. He found out the brakes had been tampered with."

Abe frowned at her. "The brakes? I don't remember anything after we left home to go to dinner."

"That's not unusual, Abe." They both looked as John Thompson stood at the foot of the bed. "Our minds will cover up incidents like that as a protective measure. How are you feeling today?"

"Ready to go home, but not ready to run a marathon."

John laughed. "That would not be a good idea for either of you. Murphy's waiting for you, and he has the whole team with him."

"The whole team? I wouldn't think that was necessary."

"He seems to think it is. He has both your work vehicles here. He's taking no chances."

Murphy turned as Abe and Emma walked towards him. He winced at the colour on their faces but thanked God for His protection the night before. It could have been so much worse.

"Ready to go home?"

Emma nodded. "I'm ready to go home and do some more research. I hope Jace has more data for me."

"Emma, John has strictly said no computer use for a day or two. He's worried you may have suffered a concussion last night."

"I've been there, done that, and it's not true today. Abe maybe, but not me."

"Stop speaking for me, Emma. I can talk for myself."

Emma glared at Abe. "Would you care to have a fight right here, right now, Mr. Finlay?"

Murphy stared at the two, wondering what had happened. He didn't know that the two had come up with a plan to stage a public fight, hoping word would get back to Charlie.

"Not happening, Emma. Now, let's move. Murphy and the guys are waiting for us."

"Don't order me around. I'll move when I'm ready to."

Abe grasped her arm and pulled her towards the door. "Let's go, Emma. We're not sick enough to be here."

Murphy trailed behind them, brows together as he tried to figure out what was going on. He raised his eyes to meet Ian's and shook his head.

Later that afternoon, Abe went searching for Emma, knowing she'd be at work. She was in the office, head cradled on her arms on the desktop as she slept. He reached around her to pick up the material she had been working on. He stopped, shocked at what she had discovered. He shot her a look, then turned to walk away. He heard a tap on the front door and headed that way.

"Murphy, Micah. Just who I needed to see. Come into the kitchen. Emma's asleep in the office, and I was just about to put on a pot of coffee. Emma's found a wealth of information for us." He handed it to Murphy, who scanned through it, then handed it to Micah.

"How does she do it?" Murphy asked.

Abe shrugged. "I have no idea, but she and Jace can drag up information like I've never seen anyone else do. No offence, Micah."

"So, where do we go with this?" Murphy's mind was working to determine a course they could follow.

"That's what we'll need to discuss. I'm going to call Frankie and Eddie and see if they can meet us out here. Frankie called a while ago. The brakes were definitely tampered with. He still can't figure out how we ended up not killed."

"God had protection around you two last night." Micah took the cup of coffee Abe offered him. "Where do you want to meet?"

"The living room, I think. There's Eddie and Frankie now. The other guys are on their way as well."

Eddie stared at Abe for a minute as he put forward a plan. "I don't like it, Abe. He almost killed you two last night."

"Do we know for sure it was him?" Abe's question stopped them.

"We don't, Abe. That's the thing. We're assuming it was him, but there is no evidence to back it up." Frankie was frustrated.

"That's the way he's always worked." Abe handed over the material Emma had collated. He had made copies for the two detectives. "Take this and work it through.

Emma's been able to prove he's been involved in more than one suspicious death. Police departments are now looking at every one of those women and their deaths. He's on borrowed time."

"And his borrowed time includes getting rid of you two and taking over Emma's trust fund and her shares." Luke spoke up.

"He can't get to the money or the shares. It's already been transferred."

"Did Emma have a birthday we didn't know about?" Eddie's thoughts went to his wife. Peg would be sorry to have missed it.

"She did, two days ago. She didn't want to celebrate, knowing it would draw attention to her and bring him out of the woodwork after her."

"That's why you had your accident last night." Ian's voice had a bite to it, one it only had when he was angry. "He's found out about that and is determined to make her pay."

"That's what we figured out today. Our only option now is to try and find him. He'll be found. Emma's put out the word on the street that she wants him. Tony has also left men here in town, who are searching for him."

"Tony?" Frankie was surprised but knew he shouldn't be.

"Yes, Tony." Emma spoke from the doorway. "He promised he'd look after me, years ago, as he promised Abe's father. This is his way of keeping his promise. You won't find his men. I probably wouldn't be able to either."

Eddie turned as she spoke. "Tony?"

"Antonio Marchionda."

"Now, that's interesting, Emma, that you know him."

She shrugged. "I had dealings with him a few years ago. He's changed. Abe's father did as well."

Abe felt Eddie's eyes on him and shrugged. "So, where do we go from here?"

Emma sat on the arm of Abe's chair. "I would suggest we continue as we have been. Eddie and Frankie will continue working through the ream of material we've given them, searching for clues and details. Your team will continue with their training. The only thing I ask is that I research your contacts for those coming in for training. It would be easy for him to sneak a team in and take out your team before you could do anything, Abe.”

The men exchanged glances. “That’s what we’re afraid of, Emma.” Ian spoke up. “Micah researches our clients, but we have found in the past that they have hidden agendas. Gideon’s on board with that as well. Now that you’re here, I know you’ll be doing that. Three pairs of eyes are good, until we catch this fellow.”

Micah nodded. “I can’t do the in-depth research that I need to do to clear everyone. I appreciate you and Gideon doing that.” He turned to Abe. “Where do we stand, anyway?”

“The team that was coming in next week won’t be. They’re connected to a mob family, as Emma has found out for us.” Abe sighed, suddenly feeling old and tired. “If that’s all, guys, let’s pick it up in a day or so. Thanks for being there for us.”

Chapter 10

Luke studied the rocks around their compound, feeling someone watching them. He turned to find Joseph standing beside him.

"You feel it too, don't you, Luke?"

"I do, Joseph. I'm thinking we need to go up there and do a search. We haven't in a while."

"I agree. Micah and Nathaniel are free this afternoon. The four of us should be able to cover some of the ground. I would say whoever it is would be close to us, not back too far."

Luke nodded. "I agree. Let's head out right after lunch."

Searching the area, they came up empty. There was nothing to show anyone had been there for a while, but they knew someone had.

"Whoever it is has covered their tracks well." Micah was frustrated.

"They have. Let's search a little further out. They may have been back farther than we thought," Joseph responded.

A sudden yell from Nathaniel had them moving his way at a rapid pace. He was staring at the ground and looked up as they approached.

"He was right here, guys. And had a direct line of sight to Abe's kitchen. He could have taken them out at any time." He pointed to the evidence he had found.

"I'll call in Frankie and his team. Who gets to tell Abe and Emma?" Luke looked up to see eyes on him. "I guess I'm nominated."

The other three men smiled. "You'd be guessing right."

Abe turned as the four men walked into his kitchen, not liking the looks on his face.

"What did you find?"

"Someone's been up in the rocks again, Abe." Nathaniel was angry that this was happening again. "How do they keep getting up there without us seeing them?"

Abe shrugged. "I have no idea, except we can't put security up there. It's just too big an area. Frankie's team is on their way, I gather?"

Micah nodded. "They are. He's not happy that we found this."

"I didn't expect he would be. When I talked to him this morning, he said they're making progress in the material, but it's taking time to work through it all and verify it."

A sudden streak of fur had the four men staring at the floor, then watching as a kitten scaled its way up Abe's leg and shirt to sit on his shoulder. It reached to wash his ear and when he blocked that, to wash his hair.

"Meow Too, enough already." His hand cupped the little calico kitten to keep her still.

"Uh, Abe. You have a kitten on your shoulder. When did you get it?" Micah had a hard time controlling his laughter and he knew the other three men were the same.

"Emma found her downtown yesterday and came home with her. She's supposed to be Emma's kitten."

"I would say she's yours, by the looks of it." Luke laughed at the expression on Abe's face.

"If that's Meow Two, where's Meow One?" Nathaniel had a grin on his face as he looked around, then back at the kitten, who by this time had decided she needed a bath, every few licks getting Abe's ear.

Abe laughed, startling the little creature. "There's no Meow One. She doesn't meow, only purrs. Emma keeps telling her she can meow too."

The men broke out in laughter at that. "That's quite the name."

"And rest assured, it will change." Emma walked into the kitchen and reached for the kitten, cuddling her close, then heading for the laundry room, closing the door to keep the kitten in it. "What did I hear about you finding evidence in the rocks?"

"We did. Frankie's on his way out with the team."

Emma nodded. "I can tell you that he won't find much, and that it was not likely Charlie." She turned around to face them. "I have found new evidence and I am glad Frankie's on his way out." She turned to walk away, and Abe caught her by her wrist.

"What new evidence?" The two stared at each other, silent communication going on between them.

She nodded. "Tony's been in touch, and I've verified what he told me. Charlie had hired a sniper in the past, which is likely who was taking potshots at your guys, Abe. The thing is, from what we can determine, and Jace has been working on this as well, it's a female sniper."

"That's what Lydia said, too, that a female could get in and out and change appearance." Luke was frustrated. "How do we find a female?"

"Tony's given me a couple of names that he knows of. Word is out that we're looking for her, so she'll go underground. Once we have the pictures, we'll pass them on to Eddie or Frankie and have them do a press conference." Emma turned as Abe touched her arm.

"That might not work as well as you hope."

She shrugged. "I know, Abe, but I refuse to live in fear any more. He took ten years from us. I refuse to give him more than the month Tony said we had. And that month is almost up."

Abe nodded, then looked at the four men standing in his kitchen, and then at the other three who had just entered. Frankie and

Eddie were behind them. "We need to make some plans, Emma, not just wing it."

She turned, frustrated. "I know that, Abe. I know we have to make plans. And if he's figured out his dates, he'll be trying to access the trust funds and shares. When he finds he can't, that will set him off even more."

"Just a minute, Emma." Eddie walked towards her. "Your birthday is past, isn't it?"

She nodded. "I set it up for everything to disappear from the bank to another bank overnight that day. He would have to search long and hard and deep to find them. Even then, he can't touch them."

Eddie nodded. "So we can expect an escalation in his violence towards you. How do we keep you two safe?"

Abe shook his head. "The same way we did with the other men. And before Ian even suggests it, we're not running."

Emma spun to stare at him, then back at Ian. "I've heard he offers to spirit people away."

Ian grinned. "That I do. I know a lot of places people can hide for days on end."

"You always offered that before we got married, Ian. I don't think it will work now." Nathaniel shook his head at him.

"Not likely, though we could always try."

Emma smiled at their nonsense. "Maybe, as a last resort. But, Charlie is here in town. I would suspect he has changed his appearance by now." She turned to Frankie. "Here's more information on him that we've dug up. If we could only catch him, so many people could go on with their lives, not living with the knowledge that something happened to their loved ones they can't prove."

Frankie kept his eyes on her as he took the material. "How much more are you going to dig up?"

"As much as I can. We've reached the end of the parameters I set. If needed, we can go past that."

"Why don't we work with what we have right now?" Frankie shared a glance with Abe. "If we need to we can search further."

"Let Frankie work with what he has for now, Emma. You said you had to testify in

court next week. You need to be getting
ready for that."

She waved her hand in dismissal. "It's
all ready."

Chapter 11

Murphy watched as Abe paced the business office, then shared a glance with Ian and Joseph, a frown on his face. This was not Abe, to be so preoccupied.

"Abe, talk to us. Tell us what's up." Ian's voice broke into Abe's concentration.

Abe sighed softly to himself, then turned to face his three friends. "I don't like the thought of Emma off by herself next week to testify. It's only for a few hours, she says, but still, anything can happen."

"What day is it she had to be there and where?"

"It's in Greentown, and on Tuesday. Some of us have to be here, myself included."

Murphy rose from his seat and walked towards the assignment board. "I'm free, as are Nathaniel and Joseph. We could head over with her."

"She won't like that, Murphy." Abe was shaking his head.

"Tough. It's how we'll play it."

Abe grinned at him. "You'll have a fight on your hand, Murphy."

Murphy shook his head. "I don't think so." He turned his head as Emma entered the office, a folder in her hand. "We've already come to an agreement."

"An agreement, Murphy? And what would that be?" Emma absentmindedly commented.

"That you've agreed to let some of us go with you next week when you testify."

She looked up and blinked at him. "I did?"

Ian nodded. "You did."

She shrugged. "If I did, I did, I guess. I don't like it though."

Abe stared at his wife, astonishment on his face, until she winked at him. He then laughed. "I might have known. You've had it all arranged already."

Tuesday, Emma leafed through her notes, then tucked them away in her briefcase. She was not comfortable traveling to another town, even though three of Abe's men were with her.

Murphy watched her in the rearview mirror, then his eyes were caught by a vehicle following them. The windows were shaded and he couldn't see how many men were inside. Joseph picked up his unease and glanced behind him as well.

"So, tell me, gentlemen, do we have a shadow?" Emma's voice cut through the silence in the van.

"We do, but how did you know?" Joseph stared at her from where he was seated beside her.

"It's a give-a-way when you keep looking behind you. Tell me, is the vehicle black, darkened windows, personalized plate?"

Murphy shot her a glance, then spoke, "How did you know?"

"I figured Tony would send his men. He seems to know a lot about where I'm heading."

Nathaniel turned to watch her in a thoughtful manner. "How would he know you were heading there today?"

She shrugged. "I didn't tell him, but he has a huge network of friends and acquaintances who keep him on top of what's going on. I can safely say, with what Abe and

I are going through, he has put out word all over that he wants to know what we're up to."

"And you're okay with that?" Murphy spoke, knowing who Tony had been in the past.

Emma shrugged. "Tony will never hurt me, Abe, or any one of you or your wives. That extends to your families as well. Once he knew I was part of Rebel's, he extended his protection to us all. That's who he is."

The three men exchanged glances, then shook their heads. They had never been part of something like that before.

Emma's phone chimed, and she pulled it out. As she read the text, her face paled.

"Murphy, find somewhere to pull over that is in a wide-open space. We need to stop."

"If we stop, we'll be late to the court."

Emma sighed. "It's not going to matter now, anyway. The person I was to testify against has been killed in an accident, and I just got word from the prosecutor there's a bomb threat at the courthouse."

Joseph and Nathaniel turned to her, as Murphy searched for a place to stop. He pulled into the parking lot of a mall and stopped, turning to her.

"A bomb threat?"

She nodded. "That's right. I won't need to testify." Her mind was racing. "But this smells like a setup. If we turn around and head right back home, Charlie will have someone waiting for us."

The three men stared at her, then at each other. Her thought processes amazed them.

"Okay, so what do we do?" Joseph watched as she thought it through.

"I have no idea. That's your specialty, isn't it?"

They took a look at her, then smiled. She was trying to lighten the day, but they could see the worry. She had her phone out and missed their looks.

"Abe? No, I'm fine, sweetheart, but there's been a change in plans. If you'd let me explain, I'd tell you. No, I don't need you to come get me. Abe! Listen, will you? Sweetheart, I'm not mad at you, but I need to speak. So, this is what's up. I won't be testifying after all. That person was killed in an accident. There's also been a bomb threat at the courthouse. Right now, we're sitting in a mall parking lot trying to think through what to do. I don't know, that's what we're working on. If we turn right around, I have a sense that Charlie or his men will be waiting on the way home."

Abe paced as he listened to Emma's voice and her words. She was right. He couldn't leave to go find her, not with the team in training.

Emma watched as the car that had been following them pulled up next to them. The three men watched it. Before they could stop her, she was out of the vehicle and walking towards the car. The door opened and a younger man stepped out, waiting for Emma to approach.

Murphy was out of their vehicle and behind her, reached for her arm to stop her.

"Emma, wait. Don't ever do that again."

She shrugged of his hand. "I know this man, Murphy. He's Tony's son."

Murphy hesitated, then kept pace with her. "I'm not leaving you, so don't try anything."

"I didn't think you would. But I know Tony Jr. He won't hurt me. I need you to stay back a bit, please, Murphy."

Murphy stopped and watched as Emma and Tony Jr. spoke. After a few minutes, Emma walked back towards Murphy.

"Get rid of your mad, Murphy. I've had enough of it already."

Murphy grabbed her arm and almost shoved her into the vehicle. "Don't ever do that again, Emma. You're under our protection. How do we face Abe if something happens to you on our watch?"

She glared back at him. "Then, I guess I won't be under your care anymore, will I? I will not be restricted in what I do or where I go?"

The two other men watched the silent battle going on between the two until Murphy slid behind the wheel and drove off, heading for home, Tony Jr.'s vehicle behind them.

"What did you say to him, Emma?" Nathaniel's quiet question broke the frigid silence in the vehicle.

She turned her gray eyes on him and shook her head. "Just that we were heading home."

The men knew there was more to it than that but didn't push. They would let Abe deal with her.

Abe shook his head when Murphy approached him later that day. "She's been on her own for so long, she doesn't realize the effect her actions can have."

"No, I don't think it's that, Abe. She's made a decision on how she wants to proceed. She needs to let us in on it. Otherwise, we can't keep her or you, for that matter, safe."

Abe stared past Murphy. "She has. She's determined to find Charlie and bring him down." He turned as the door opened, and Emma entered.

"Abe, I just figured out something. I don't like it."

"And that would be?"

Emma headed for the white board and started listing Abe's team and their duties on the board:

Matt - paramedic - car accident

Nathaniel - sniper -

Murphy - negotiations - envelope in car

Ian - paralegal -

Joseph - security -

Luke - armaments - bomb threat at courthouse

Micah - computer expert -

"He's targeting us by picking and choosing which of your team he'll go after in this way. He's going to work through them all until he gets to you, as the leader."

Murphy and Abe stared at the board, then turned to watch her.

"How'd you come up with that, Emma?" Murphy's voice was quiet as he tried to follow her thought processes.

She shrugged. "Something had been bothering me since this all started. It was the bomb threat today. I had mentioned to Luke that we might need his expertise when I found out what he does on the team." She turned to Abe, distress on her face. "How do we stop him, Abe, before one of your guys or their ladies get hurt, or even killed?"

Murphy headed out to find the rest of their team. A meeting was in order, he thought.

Abe reached to pull Emma into his arms. Holding her tight, he rested his chin on her head. "I don't know, sweetheart. Murphy's gone to get the team." He pulled back enough he could see her face. "What's this I hear you did today?"

"Murphy was not happy. I knew the car, Abe, and I knew Tony would have left close family or friends to watch us. I know I shouldn't have walked over there, but there was no way your guys would have let me. I needed to talk to him." She leaned back into him.

"Murphy said you wouldn't say what you talked about." He felt her shake her head.

"I couldn't until I talked to you. Tony said his father wants those two to stay close to us. He's trying to do what his father wants, but it's difficult where we live out here. He's searching town for Charlie and his henchmen as well."

Abe hugged her tight again. "That's okay. Just don't do it again. For all you knew, that could have been Charlie in that car."

"I knew it wasn't. Tony sent me a text message when we were sitting there."

"A text message?"

She nodded, not seeing the looks on the faces of the three men who had been with her. "He's got his finger in so many places. He heard about the bomb threat and wanted me to talk with his son."

"And how do you know his son isn't involved with Charlie?"

Emma sighed and pulled away from Abe, stopping as she saw the team watching her. "I guess I have to break a confidence, don't I?" She turned back to Abe. "I knew your father had helped Tony. We talked about it once, back when I was helping him. What you never knew is that Tony Jr. was kidnapped as a young boy. When they found out where he was being held, Tony approached your Dad to go in and get him. Your Dad went in on his own and found him and got him out."

Abe stared at her, then lifted his eyes to his team, who stood in shocked silence. "Dad helped a mobster?"

Emma nodded, her eyes on her husband. "He did. Tony had to persuade him to do so, but he said something along the lines that your father had prayed hard about it and having a son himself, he couldn't say no." She sighed, eyes on the floor. "Tony Jr. has sworn that he would do everything he could to help your Dad or you if the time ever came. He was never involved in his Dad's activities. In fact, until Tony changed, Tony Jr. stayed away from him."

"God works in mysterious ways, Abe. He has a plan and purpose we don't see." Murphy's favourite words flowed through the office. "I'm sorry I was so harsh, Emma. I didn't know."

She turned to him. "I'm sorry. I should have talked to you first. I'm just so used to doing things on my own. I'm learning." She pointed at the board. "Now about that."

The men turned to the board and she could see the concern rippling through them.

"How'd you do that, Emma?" Ian's voice was tight.

She shrugged. "I can't explain it, Ian. It's just how my mind works."

"Yep, scary Emma strikes again." Murphy grinned at her. "Now, where do we go from here? And how does the envelope come in?"

"Frankie finally told me what was in the envelope. It was a threat against me and Abe." She turned to Abe. "Frankie said he talked to you too."

Abe nodded. "He did. Their team is working through the massive amount of material you gave them. He asked if you could hold off on any more, unless you were really certain it would help move the investigation."

Emma nodded. "Jace has some more that will. He's to meet with Eddie or Frankie this afternoon."

Chapter 12

Abe was on a hunt. Emma wasn't in the house or the business office. Now, where was she, he thought? His eyes turned to the lake at the back of the property and he headed that way. Joseph looked up as he walked by him and pointed at a rock formation. Abe nodded his thanks and angled that way.

Emma was perched in a sheltered area where no one would have seen her. Her face was pensive, but there was a lingering sadness he could see.

Stopping in front of her, he touched, her foot, causing her to jump.

"Sorry, sweetheart, didn't mean to scare you."

She shook her head. "No, it's okay. It's just everything is overwhelming today."

Abe leaned against the rock, his eyes of her face. "We all have days like that. Care to share?"

She searched his face and eyes. "I just have this feeling of trouble and doom coming down on us." She brushed away a tear that fell. "I also found this, and I'm not sure where we go from here." She handed him a paper she had had crumpled in her hand.

Abe took it, his eyes on her face. "It's that bad?"

She nodded. "Read it and then we'll talk."

Abe dropped his eyes to the paper. His heart stilled at what she had been able to dig up.

"I see you've been researching again. How did you come up with this?"

She shrugged. "I can never explain it, Abe. I've tried, and I just can't."

"So, you think this fellow is involved?"

"Absolutely. Tracking back names, he would be Charlie's son, born before he started all this with his black widower days."

"And have you found out where he is?"

She sighed, shivered, and then nodded. "He'll be in town. He's likely working with Charlie. Or if he's working on his own, we now have two sets of people to watch for. He's likely the one who broke into my house.

He's been convicted of numerous break and enters and thefts."

Abe reached up and pulled her down to him, wrapping her in his arms. "I guess we'll need to go find Frankie."

"I already called and spoke with Eddie. He's not happy with what I dug up.

"Didn't think he would be. Come on, sweetheart. We need to talk to our team."

"What I really need, Abe, is a couple of days away so I can go fly with the eagles."

Abe stopped, a thought crossing his mind. "Did you take that picture in your office?"

She nodded, a smile crossing her face. "I did. I think Matt and Nathaniel were in the office talking to Jace when I got it." She stopped walking, lost in thought, reliving the moment she captured the picture. "I'd been trying for years to get it and that day, they were within ten feet of me. I had told Jace that if I ever got the picture of an eagle I wanted, my life would straighten out."

Abe smiled. "And then a few weeks later, I walked into your office."

Emma looked up. "Frankie's here. I just don't want to talk to him."

"Unfortunately, you have to." Abe turned in a circle as he assessed the area around him. "I can feel someone watching us, Emma. We're too much in the open here."

She nodded, a grin crossing her face. "Race you!" She took off at a run, leaving Abe standing staring at her for a moment, before he gave a shout of laughter and chased after her.

"How was that, sweetheart?" Emma was laughing as he caught her in his arms and swung her in a circle.

"Next time, warn me you can run so fast." He grinned down at her, then looked up as Frankie approached.

"Abe. Emma. Can we go somewhere we can talk?" A grim look on his face drove the smiles from both their faces.

Abe pointed at the business office. "Do I need to find my team?"

Frankie stared at him, then stared around the compound. "It would likely be best. They're going to need to be in on our planning."

Abe's team scattered throughout the business office, finding seats, eyes on Frankie.

Emma in Abe's chair, he stood behind her, hands on her shoulders.

"Okay, Frankie. We're all here. What have you discovered?"

Frankie stared at Emma, trying to assess how she came up with the names she did. "How did you find that name, Emma?" His voice was brisk and a little harsh.

She jerked at the tone of his voice, eyes narrowing as she stared back. "Don't question my methods, Frankie, or next time you don't get the information. I'll pass it on to someone else and leave you out of it totally."

"The thing is, Emma, you can't do that. I'm the investigating officer." Frankie returned her stare.

"I can and will, Frankie. I have already spoken to Caleb about this."

Abe's hands tightened on her shoulders. What was up with these two?

"Be it as it may, I am still the investigator until Caleb removes me. Tell me, how did you come up with this name?" He raised the sheet of paper in his hands.

"I cannot and will not discuss my methods. That is a confidential program that

I share with no one. As to how, I just kept researching Charlie, finding multitudes of names he uses, until I came to that name.” She pointed at his piece of paper. “You should be thanking me, instead of making me feel like a criminal.” She was up and out of the office before any of the men could stop her.

Abe stared after her, then turned hard, angry eyes on his friend. “This has to stop, Frankie. Emma’s not the criminal here.”

“And how do you know that?” Frankie wasn’t backing down.

“Because I know her. As of now, this conversation is over. You need to leave, Frankie. When you can discuss this in a civilized manner, come back.” Abe turned and walked away, searching for his wife.

His team shared a look, then stared at Frankie. Frankie shook his head and without a word, walked away

“Well, that was interesting,” Ian commented. “What was that all about?”

Abe opened the office door, peered in, and then entered. “I take it Frankie wasn’t happy?”

His friends stared at him.

"Not really, Abe. Care to explain?" Murphy knew something was up, but wasn't sure what.

Abe nodded. "Emma found a son of Charlie from his very first marriage. He's into criminal activity and is here in the area. He's either working with his father or working on his own. Apparently, Frankie doesn't believe Emma." Abe paused, eyes assessing his men. "We need to think this through and then make plans."

"So, what do we do? And have you a picture of him?" Joseph was thinking ahead to what he knew had to be done.

"Here, this is what he looked like six months ago. He's likely changed his appearance by now." Emma had entered the office and was handing each man a picture of the son. "His name is Wayne Jones. He doesn't share the same name as Charlie. It looks as if his parents divorced and Wayne took his mother's name. That doesn't mean he isn't using Charlie's name of West."

Micah shook his head. "Caleb was right, Emma. You are scary. I can find a lot of information and so can Kat, but you have us beat."

She smiled. "Thank you, Micah. That means a lot." She searched the faces of the men staring at her. "So, what kind of plans are we making? When do you have to be away again? I have another court appearance in two weeks, unless she pleads."

Abe drew her down into a chair. "That's what we were just discussing. We have a team in for training Monday to Thursday next week. The following week, we've been asked to provide security for Tuesday and Wednesday in Oak City." He searched the men's faces, seeing the grimness in them. "How do we do it, guys?"

"Call in Don Woods. He'll help." Luke spoke up, naming a security team leader that was good friends with Abe.

"He would, I know."

Emma turned her eyes on Abe, frown in place. "You can trust this man?"

"We can, sweetheart. He's a good friend as is his team. Paul, on his team, steps in if we need someone to help out. Don came in and provided security for Micah and Kat not that long ago. And I know you'll research them. They have really high government security. That doesn't just happen."

She nodded. "Okay, so your team's away. What do I do?"

"Live in the safe room?" Ian stared back at the look she gave him, a small grin lurking on his face.

"Absolutely not, Ian. I don't do that, especially in a room underground." She turned to watch each of the men. "So, what do we do? I know I'm not going to like it, not one bit."

That comment caused the men to start to laugh, and Emma spun in her chair to throw a questioning look at Abe.

"It's okay, sweetheart. All the ladies said the same thing, that they didn't like it."

She shrugged. "So, I'm part of the in crowd then, am I?" A slight smile crossed her face and then she bit her lip. "How do we do it then, guys?"

"Don Woods will step in the two days we're away. That won't be a problem. Nathaniel's already talked to him." He studied the board she had listed the team on. "One thing, though, worries me. Which one of our duties will be next?"

Matt spoke up. "I would say security. If we're away and he hasn't made a move before then, that's when he will. We've already found evidence of them in the rocks."

"Or I could go fly with my eagles when you're away." Emma had a small smile on her face as she looked at Abe.

"Not without me, you're not. Not anymore." He looked over as the door opened, and Caleb walked in.

"Caleb? What are you doing out here?" Abe was surprised. Caleb very seldom came his way during the day.

Caleb studied Emma for a moment, then lifted his eyes to Abe. "I understand Emma's not happy with Frankie?"

"No, I'm not, Caleb. No one questions my integrity or my work."

He nodded. "I know that. Frankie does, too. He's just not seeing how you're finding what you're finding."

"You've had opportunity work with me before, Caleb. You know I find things and can't explain how." Emma was refusing to back down from the police investigators.

"We have, Emma, and we have you as a consultant for us. This time, though, you're the one at risk, and we need to make sure that what evidence we have isn't compromised when we go to court."

"We won't be going to court, not for us, Caleb. That's the thing of it. He's wanted in too many places for murder and attempted murder, we'll never get to him for what he did to Abe and I."

The security team exchanged glances with one another. They knew what she meant. Their eyes then tuned to Caleb, stopping as they caught the look on Abe's face.

Abe studied his wife. "You're sure on that, Emma?"

She nodded. "I am, Abe. I have tracked him back to at least eight to ten murders, that many more possible." Abe's hands tightened on her shoulders. "Then, there's the bank fraud as well."

"I can see why he wants you out of the way, Emma, in addition to the trust funds you moved." Matt's eyes moved from Emma to Abe to Caleb.

Caleb blew out a breath of frustration as he sat. "I know all this, Emma, but you need to work with us."

"I won't work with Frankie any more, Caleb. He's called my integrity into question, and I don't allow that."

"Then, how do you meet him on a personal level? He's good friends with Abe."

She shrugged. "We'll have to work on that, I guess, but not on a professional level. If that's all you've come to say, I'm done." Abe's hands on her shoulders kept her in his chair.

"I don't think it is, Emma. I know Caleb too well."

"You're right, Abe. It isn't the only reason I'm here." Caleb's speech stopped and he stared at Abe. "We found Charlie's son this morning."

"You found him?"

Caleb nodded. "He's in hospital, but not expected to survive. That changes what we need to do. Evidence suggests that Charlie was present when his son was stabbed."

"No, that doesn't fit with Charlie's character. Drugging people, like he did me, yes. Having people beaten and killed, yes. But there is no way he'd do the deed himself. He wouldn't want to sully his lily-white fingers."

"We don't think he actually did the deed himself. We think the men he has hired have done it. If this is the case, then he is taking out his competition in trying to get to you."

Emma waved her hands in the air. "Just a minute. Whoever said Wayne was after us? We may have thought that, and considered him as breaking into my home, but we had no proof."

"Unfortunately, we don't have proof, and we not likely will ever have that proof." Caleb studied the floor in front of his feet. "Work with us, Emma. We need your expertise on this."

She stood, shaking off Abe's hands. "You know my answer on that one, Caleb. Professionally, I will not work with Frankie. He's got something going on, and he doesn't trust me. I can't work with that lack of trust."

Abe stared as Emma walked away, then caught a movement from Luke.

"Luke?" Abe's eyebrow raised as he asked the question.

"Unfortunately, she's right, Abe. We've picked that up from day one. He doesn't trust her, not like he should. Not like we do, or Eddie or Caleb do. We've talked about it among ourselves and can't figure it out." Luke looked as his fellow teammates as he spoke. "We're not sure what the answer is, but their conflict is there, and we can see it affecting the investigation from Frankie's point of view. He has never really accepted what she has to say."

"It likely comes back to the fact of what happened all those years ago and that she didn't try to find you, Abe." Murphy had thought it through and talked it over with Adriel. "I don't think he believes what she's saying, even though she's provided proof."

Caleb sighed as he stood. "I'll talk with him, Abe, but I think I'll need to remove him and put Jake Wilson on it. Frankie's been pulling in too many hours without a break."

"He needs a to take a break, Caleb. He's burning out, just like he did when he was undercover." Abe spoke up, knowing that Caleb had already realized that.

Caleb shared a look with Abe. "You're right, all of you. He shouldn't be reacting the way he is with Emma. He never did in the past with your team."

Joseph hesitated before he spoke. "I think he's afraid she'll walk on Abe again, and he doesn't want to see that happen. That is no excuse for what we've seen over the course of the last few weeks. He's been out of line on more than one occasion with Emma, and she's called him on it."

Abe nodded. "She has, Caleb. She will not tolerate someone questioning her like Franke did. To tell you the truth, neither will I."

Caleb nodded as he turned to the door. "I'll talk with him. As of now, Jake Wilson will be the lead investigator. With Eddie as your uncle, Abe, we can't have him as lead, just in case someone questions that."

"Is Sue still working investigations?"

Caleb turned to Murphy. "She is. If Jake can't handle it, I'll call in Sue, but Jake has come so far in his skills.

Chapter 13

Caleb looked up from his desk as a knock came to his door. Frankie stood there, hesitant in his manner.

"Come in, Frankie. Shut the door, please." Caleb looked down at his desk as Frankie sat in one of the chairs in front of him.

"I can guess what this is about, Caleb."

Caleb's keen eyes studied Frankie. "Can you? How about you talk to me, then, about what's going on with you and Emma?"

Frankie shook his head. "I have no idea, Caleb. I just don't trust her."

Caleb sat back. "That unfortunate, Frankie, seeing as Abe is a good friend of yours. You need to figure out why you don't trust her when everyone else does. You've worked with her before without an issue. Why the problem now?"

Frankie's eyes studied the pattern on the floor. "I don't know, Caleb. I just don't know."

"I had a talk with both Emma and Abe today. They're concerned about you as is his team. You're not acting like yourself." Caleb paused to watch Frankie's face. "I am too, Frankie. You're not yourself. Talk to me."

Frankie shook his head. "I don't know what it is, Caleb."

Caleb nodded. "Then, if you don't or won't or can't tell me why you have such an issue with Emma, I need to replace you as head investigator." Frankie's eyes shot to him at that. "I understand you haven't had a vacation in quite a while. It's time you and your wife took off for a week or two. Go, find somewhere you can relax, spend some time with Deirdre, and most importantly, time with God. When you come back, I want to hear that you're meeting with Greg Evans on a regular basis. You're getting beaten up again, Frankie. I don't want to lose you to the detective squad."

Frankie hesitated. "I guess I need to do some fence mending, is what you're saying, Caleb. I have no idea why I feel like I do."

"Joseph had an interesting observation. He thinks that you're feeling that Emma will walk on Abe again"

Frankie looked startled, then his eyes slid shut. "He's right, you know. I just can't accept what happened."

"You need to figure that out, Frankie. Knowing the character of who we're after should tell you that Emma is an innocent victim in this. I've spoken with Jace. Jace found her on the streets of his city about a month after she ran. He said she was extremely sick when he picked her up and carried her back to his mother. She almost didn't make it." Frankie's eyes were steady on Caleb at this point. "From what I can understand, she was mourning the loss of Abe, and really didn't care what happened to her. Jake's traced back the information her uncle provided to the man who made it up for him. He's been wanting to talk to you, but you have kept putting him off. Emma and Abe have been through more than most people, and you know what you went through with Deirdre."

Frankie nodded. "Deirdre's been after me to take some time off. I guess it's for the best."

"Before you go, Frankie, let's pray together. We haven't had a chance to do that in a long time, and we need it. Then, you need to go make your peace with both Abe and Emma. Abe's pretty upset with you."

"And well he should be."

Finger marking his place in his book, Abe answered the door to find Frankie standing there. He stepped aside to let Frankie in, watching his hesitant manner.

"Abe, can I talk to you and Emma?"

"Frankie, come in and have a seat. Emma's already retired."

Frankie sighed. "I was hoping to speak with her tonight. Deirdre and I are heading out tomorrow morning for a vacation."

"It's time you took one, Frankie. You've been pushing too hard over the last few months, and you're almost to the point you were when you had to take time off before. I don't like to see that in you." Abe studied his friend. "What did you want to speak with her about?"

"I need to apologize, both to her and to you, Abe. I let my feelings get in the way of a proper investigation. She was right to call me on it."

Abe nodded, his eyes tracing past Frankie to the stairway, where Emma stood. "Just a moment, Frankie." He stood and went to where Emma was standing. "Emma?"

"I heard Frankie's voice. I need to apologize to him, Abe. I can't sleep unless I do."

Abe drew her into a hug. "That's what he's here for too, Emma."

Frankie stood as Emma approached, Abe's arm around her. "Emma, I'm sorry. I have had no reason for how I've acted, other than that I was afraid Abe would end up alone again."

Emma studied the man standing in front of her. "Apology accepted, Frankie. Just don't even question me about my work or my integrity. If you need to speak with me, please do so in a civilized manner or speak with me privately."

Frankie breathed a sigh of relief. "That I will, Emma. I can see how well you two are suited, and I was just afraid."

"You've said that, Frankie. It's now in the past as far as I am concerned. I need to apologize to you as well. I was harsh in my words, not like I usually am."

"Apology accepted. Listen, I can't stay. Deirdre and I are heading out in the morning. Caleb's kicked me out of the office for a couple of weeks." He turned, eyes shadowed once again. "Emma, Abe, I can't tell you how sorry I am. Caleb explained what Jace had found, that I was too busy to find out."

"You've been driven for too long, Frankie. You pour yourself into any investigation, particularly if it involves a friend. You need to learn how to step back and review what's happening. Find yourself someone who will call you on that in the future." Emma's compassionate eyes rested on Frankie's face. "I look forward to working with you again."

"Caleb's put Jake on lead for your investigation. That's what needed to be done. I was too close to you two."

Abe turned to Emma after he had locked the door. "What are you thinking, Emma?"

She looked up at him, a faraway look in her eyes. She brought her attention back to Abe, who was standing in front of her, a puzzled look on his face.

"There's something wrong here, Abe. I know Frankie has accepted it, but there's just something wrong." She spun to head for the office.

"Hold on, Emma. What do you mean, there's something wrong?"

Emma shook her head. "I can't explain it, Abe. I get these feelings sometimes and have to search."

He caught her hand. "Leave it until morning, sweetheart. It's getting late, and you have to be up early to be at the office to meet your client."

Emma's eyes flew to his and her hand covered her mouth. "That's what it is. I don't like the sounds of that new client." She grabbed for his hand and pulled him with her. "Let me do a little bit of research, okay?"

Abe shrugged, then perched on the desk as he watched her fingers fly over the keyboard. "There, Micah was the next one, not Joseph. That man I was to meet with? He's connected to Charlie."

"Warn Jace not to go in. I'll let Caleb know and they can have officers there in the office."

She searched for her phone. "Now, where did I leave it?"

Abe smiled as he handed his to her. "Likely beside the bed."

"No, I don't remember seeing it there. In fact, Abe, I haven't seen it all day."

Abe stilled. "When did you last have it?"

She shrugged. "First thing this morning."

"See if you can hear it ring." He dialed her phone, but neither one of them could hear it ringing. "Did you have it in the business office today or out by the rocks?"

"I just can't remember, Abe. I just hope it's still around and no one has gotten a hold of it."

His eyes met hers at the same thought crossed their minds. "If someone has it, they could use it, and no one would know that it wasn't me." Emma was almost in tears at the thought.

Abe watched her face. What's going on here, Lord? It's more than just a missing phone.

"I'll look for it in the morning, sweetheart. But that's not what's going on. What is it?"

She shook her head as tears began to fall. "I don't know how to tell you, Abe. I just don't know." She got up and ran from the room.

He could hear her footsteps on the stairs. *What is it, Lord?*

He grabbed a jacket and flashlight and headed for the business office. He had to check there tonight and where she had been sitting on the rocks.

Shining his light at the rocks, he reached for a shiny object he could see. Her phone! She would be so happy. He tucked it down into his pocket and turned, meeting a fist to the face as he did so.

A noise behind his assailant caused him to turn and then run for the rocks. Murphy had seen the flashes of light and headed to see what it was. He barely caught his balance as he tripped over Abe. He dropped to his knees beside him as Abe stirred.

"Abe, what are you doing out here at this time of night?"

"Looking for Emma's phone. Did you see him?"

"See who?"

"Whoever it was who nailed me. You must have scared him off."

Murphy helped Abe to his feet. "Did you get a look at him at all?"

Abe shook his head. "Just his fist."

"Let's get you back to your house, and I'll check it out. You didn't black out or anything?"

Abe shook his head, feeling his jaw. "No, he just dropped me where I stood. We'll have to come back here in the morning and see what he was up to."

Emma stood in the kitchen, staring at Abe as he handed her the phone he had found. "Abe! What were you thinking?"

"Just that I didn't want your phone in anyone's hands. Before you use it, have Joseph check it out for you."

She lifted startled eyes to his and then nodded. "Tell me, Murphy, is he okay?"

"Looks like it, Emma. He'll have a bruise, maybe, but nothing's broken. See you two in the morning."

Abe reached to lock the door behind Murphy, then turned back to Emma. "Care to explain what that was about earlier?"

She shook her head. "It's in the past, for right now. Maybe someday I can find the courage to speak about it."

"I don't like secrets, Emma. I wish you'd trust me enough to tell me."

Emma's eyes flew to him once again, and then flooded with tears. "Oh, Abe, I didn't mean it like that." She walked towards him and wrapped her arms around him. "I've had ten years to accept something that happened."

"Did anyone hurt you?" He felt her head shake against him. "Then, whatever it is, we'll deal with when you're ready to tell me."

Chapter 14

Joseph shot a look at Abe as he was handed Emma's phone. What was up, he wondered?

"Can you check it out for us, Joseph, make sure no one has tampered with it?"

"I can do that. Does she have a password?"

"Eaglet#1."

"Eaglet?" Joseph questioned Abe at the word.

"Yep. She has a thing about eagles."

"Sure, I'll check it out. Where did you say you found it?"

"On the rocks where she was sitting yesterday. That's where I ran into whoever it was lurking there."

"That's why Murphy and Nathaniel were headed that way early this morning."

Abe nodded. "They're looking to see if they can find anything. I don't think they will though."

"Where do we stand now on the investigation, Abe?" Ian spoke from the doorway.

Abe turned. "Now that Frankie's off on vacation and Jake's the lead investigator, we're pretty much starting over until Jake gets up to speed on the data." Abe was frustrated at the turn of events. Anything could happen in the meantime.

"That's not good." Ian pulled out a chart and sat. "How do we help?"

Abe shrugged. "I'm not sure what we can do. I'm not as familiar with Jake as I am with Frankie. But Caleb seemed to think it was the right move. Maybe fresh eyes will see something." He turned as Murphy and Nathaniel entered. "Find anything?"

Murphy nodded, a grim look on his face. He handed Abe an envelope.

"Not again. I was hoping this was done with." Abe turned to his team members. "I guess this means a drive into town. Who's with me?"

Nathaniel moved forward. "I am. Murphy volunteered to stay with Emma."

Abe nodded. "Thanks, guys. I'll be back soon. Meanwhile, we need to get our stuff ready for next week."

"About that, Abe," Micah spoke up. "How sure are you about that?"

Abe turned to him. "What do you mean?"

"There's just something odd about that group. I've got Jace looking into it as well."

"Keep looking. Let me know what you find out."

Jake Wilson looked up as Abe knocked at his office door. "Abe! What brings you in so early?"

"I was hoping you'd be in already." Abe studied Jake's desk, piled down with files. "Don't tell me that's all ours!"

Jake shook his head. "It's not yours at all. That's all in the conference room, and we have people sorting through it. Your wife and Jace are good, you know."

Abe smiled. "That they are. Here, Murphy and Nathaniel found this envelope this morning in some rocks where Emma likes to sit." He went on to explain what had transpired the night before.

Jake took it, his eyes on Abe. "I see you haven't opened it yet."

"No. I thought I'd let you do the honours."

Jake snorted as he reached for a pair of latex gloves and then his letter opener. "Thanks. Although I doubt this will be what you would consider an honour." He froze as he pulled out the letter and then shot a quick glance at Abe. "He's getting vicious, Abe."

"What do you mean?"

Jake pulled out an evidence bag, sealed the letter inside, and tagged it. "This. He's been close to your house, in your backyard I would say."

Abe whitened as he took the proffered bag and studied the picture and letter. "That was taken last week. My guys were in the kitchen with me." Abe stared at the picture of himself with Meow Too on his shoulder. Then, his attention turned to the letter. His heart sank as he read the words.

"You've taken my money. You will pay in a way you least expect. I'm not done with either one of you yet."

"What money is he talking about?" Jake was still trying to sort through all the data.

"Emma had trust funds from her parents and also her aunt. He wanted them. She's gotten rid of them."

"And he knows this?"

Abe nodded. "We think he does. That's what set him off ten years ago. Emma had transferred her parents' trust fund the day we got married. A few weeks ago, she transferred her aunt's."

"If you don't mind my asking, was it a lot?"

Abe nodded, his thoughts still on the letter. "It was in the millions, I'm not sure how much. There were also shares in companies that she transferred as well." He looked up at Jake. "We're likely look at twenty to thirty million."

Jake choked on his mouth of water. "That much? No wonder he's after her." He sat back and stared at Abe. "So, now what do we do?"

"My guys are staying as close to us as they can. They're worried about their wives getting caught in the crossfire, and I can't say that I blame them."

Jake nodded. "Listen, there was one thing I needed to talk to Emma about. Will she be home later today?"

"She will be." Abe hesitated, knowing he had to warn Jake. "Don't make the mistake Frankie did. She won't tolerate anyone questioning her integrity or her methods or results. Nor will I."

Jake nodded. "Totally understandable. I would have reacted the same way. How about I come out around 2?"

"I'll let her know. If we can't swing that, stop by for supper. Actually, that might be better. No one would suspect anything."

Abe grinned as Jake shook his head. "Afraid it doesn't work that way."

Jake stared at the letter after Abe left, then rose and went to find the crime tech, handing it over. He then went to find Eddie. He needed more information that what Frankie had left him and thought Eddie might be the one to help.

Jake stood watching as Emma finished off the meal. They had been talking casually waiting for Abe to come in.

"How do you enjoy working as a detective, Jake?" Emma was having a difficult time getting Jake to talk with her.

"I'm enjoying it. I've always loved to solve puzzles. Now, I get paid to do it."

Emma smiled as his analogy. "That's exactly what it is, Jake, a huge puzzle." She turned to search his face. "I know it's difficult having to pick up where Frankie left off and feel that you're up to where you need to be."

"It is, but Eddie was a great source of information. That's one thing I learned early, talk to the veterans." He turned to look out the window. "I never had a male figure in my life. Dad died when I was really young, and Mom had no brothers. My grandfathers were always too busy for me."

Emma smiled in sympathy. "And now you feel like you're floundering through life?"

Jake spun to stare at her. "How do you know that?"

"Because I have felt the very same, Jake." She looked to where Abe was standing. "Now, do we eat here or in the dining room?"

"Jake?" Abe's question caught him off guard.

"Where do you normally eat?"

Emma started to laugh. "It depends on our moods. It's usually here, though."

Abe reached past her for the plates and then cutlery. "We're not fancy here, Jake. It's usually dish up your supper from the pots and then eat."

Jake shrugged. "That's fine with me."

Jake stood, hesitating as Emma handed him a cup of coffee. She tilted her head to watch him, then glanced at Abe.

"How be we go to the living room, Jake? You said you had something to talk to Emma about."

Jake nodded, relief in his movements. "I do." When they were seated, Jake was still hesitant.

"What did you need to ask me, Jake? It can't be that hard to, I wouldn't think. I usually don't bite."

Jake shook his head as he smiled. "I know you don't. It's just so hard to understand Charlie's mindset."

"He's greedy, wants everything now, and doesn't like people in his way. If they get in his way, he gets rid of them. It's that simple." Emma paused, then continued, "He did that with Abe. Abe was an obstacle to my trust funds, so he got him out of the way, not knowing we had already taken steps. He got me out of the way, so he could deal with Abe."

Jake nodded. "That's what I don't understand. How did you get away from him?"

"One of his men helped me. He didn't like what he was being asked to do for Charlie and had planned to leave the day after I graduated. When he saw what Charlie was up to, he stayed and then helped me get way about four days after I woke up and was told Abe was dead."

"And you never looked into it?"

Emma shook her head as she reached for Abe's hand. "I was in shock, still suffering from the effects of whatever drug I had been given. I'm not even sure how he did the drug thing. Then I was really sick when Jace found me."

Jake sat back and studied her. "What about over time? Did you never wonder or never look?"

She shook her head. "I blocked a lot of that time from my mind, I think. When I did think about searching, I guess I didn't really want to know if Abe was alive and decided he didn't want anything more to do with me. Your mind can play a lot of games with you.

I can see God's hand in it all, though, His protection in everything."

Abe spoke up. "Emma's a strong person. Sometimes it's harder for them to step back and search things out. It's easier just to keep going."

Jake pulled out his notebook. "I can see that. Emma, now about your trust funds. There is no way he can get at them? He can't get you to sign them over to him?"

"Absolutely note. I have no control over them now at all. A trust company has them and is disbursing the funds. By this time next week, there will be no funds left to disburse. The shares will also be disbursed."

"So, if he knows this, he'll be working under a timeline?"

"He would have no way of knowing this. His motivation now is revenge." She looked at Abe. "That's what I'm afraid of, Jake, that he'll come after me and hurt one of the team or their wives. I couldn't live with myself if that happens."

"So, what are you now planning?"

Abe spoke up. "We're still trying to think it all through, with my team's help, but the problem is that we're busy with training and then away for a couple of days."

"And if he's watching, that's when he'll make his move."

Emma nodded. "More than likely. We also noted that he seems to know what specialty each of the guys has on the team, and what happens is linked to that."

Jake's eyes studied her. "So, he's moving through the team, until he gets to Abe." He looked down at his notes and then back up. "That's where he'll really make his move, trying to get through your protector. It's common knowledge that Abe can be very much a protector when he needs to be." He paused. "And there's no way either one of you will leave town."

"No, not without the other one. I'm determined to stay and fight this out, Jake." Emma was adamant in her words.

He nodded, then looked back down at his book. "I understand Charlie's son has died."

Emma looked stunned for a moment, then shared a look with Abe. "It's about what we figured would happen. Charlie is not a nice guy. I'm sure you caught a glimpse of all the murders he's being investigated for."

Jake stared at Emma. "I have. I don't pretend to understand how you found them, but this will bring closure to a number of families. Did you hear anything on your aunt?"

"Not yet. The coroner said it would take a bit to get definitive answers, if we even can at this point."

Jake sat back. "Talk to me, Emma. Tell me what you're feeling, what you know, what you don't know, where you plan to go from here. Eddie warned me that I might not follow all your thought processes, and Caleb told me you were scary."

Emma started to laugh. "I guess I'll never live that down, now will I? Okay, so here we go."

Jake finally tucked his notepad away in his pocket. "Thank you, Emma. This helps. Now I know what to look for in the wealth of material you've provided and that our team has dug up. Somewhere, in there, is the answer. I've put feelers out downtown, hoping someone sees him and turns him in."

Abe stood and shook Jake's hand. "Thank you, Jake. Fresh eyes may find something. Eddie's been putting in a number of hours, but Caleb is reluctant to let him do much, given we're related."

"And that could be an issue when we go to court, although I understand you don't think we will, Emma."

"Not likely, Jake, not with all the murders on the book." Emma watched as Abe walked Jake to the door, then headed for the kitchen to clean up after their meal.

Chapter 15

Tucking his paperwork back into his briefcase, Abe turned to watch his team members. Ian was at the wheel of their van, and the other ones had settled into their normal travel routine, most with a book out.

"Have you talked with Emma today, Abe?" Ian's voice was quiet.

"I have. She's doing okay, but she says she's dug up some material that we need to look at." He sighed. "I wish she'd stop finding material. It just keeps growing the case and delaying it."

Ian snickered. "That would be asking her not to breathe, you know. It's who she is and what she does."

Abe nodded, his eyes staring down the road. "She did say Don saw evidence of someone up in the rocks again. He's had two of his team stationed up there."

"I don't like that." Ian shot a quick look at Abe.

"Nor do I." Abe became lost in thought, puzzling over what they had found out. "According to Emma's chart, he's got to Micah with her searches for the teams coming in, and I would say Joseph for the way he left that envelope."

"I would too. That leaves you, me and Nathaniel. Nathaniel's is the one I'm worried about."

Abe nodded. "I know. We have confirmation that Charlie hired a sniper. We have no idea when or where."

"I would suspect somewhere there's a crowd, to cause a lot of panic. Say, church, court." Ian stopped speaking. "We may need to transport you two separately."

Abe shot him a look. "I figured as much. Emma's not going to like that."

"Whether she likes it or not, it may come to that." Ian once again stopped speaking. "It is amazing when you see how God has worked in all our lives, given what we've all gone through. He's not done with any of us yet, Abe, no matter what comes up for you two."

"No, He's not." Abe pulled his phone out as it chimed. It was Emma.

"He sent another letter. Jake's on his way out. Hurry home. Luv you. Emma"

Abe's face tightened as he read it.

"Bad news, Abe?"

Abe turned to look at Murphy. "It is. Emma just got another letter. And we're still miles from home."

"Did she let Don know?"

Abe sent a quick text back to Emma.

"Yes. He is in the house with me as is Paul. His other four men are outside, keeping a tight watch. Let the guys know their wives are off site for the day. Gideon and Rebecca left yesterday for a photo shoot and a court appearance for Gideon."

"Your wives are off site, guys, so it's just Emma and Don's men."

Abe headed for the house as soon as Ian had stopped the van. Don's men waved as they continued their patrol. Don looked up as Abe entered, then pointed to the office.

Abe stopped in the doorway to watch Emma. She hadn't heard him come in and was deep in concentration, papers spread across the desk and on the floor. Hearing a sound, she looked up, her face lighting up when she saw him.

Before she could rise, Abe was to her, dropping a kiss on her mouth in greeting.

Her hand on his arm, Emma stared up at him. "You're home. You're safe."

"That I am. And so are you." He looked around the office. "Tell me what's going on here?"

"Sorry, Abe. I had an urgent call for some information and unfortunately, it's gotten a little messy."

"That is not and never will be an issue for us. Are you almost finished?"

She looked down at her material. "An hour or less, I would think. I just have to finalize my report and send it in."

"I'll come find you then. I think we need to talk."

Emma stared at him as he walked away and then shrugged. What was with him, Lord? He's not acting like himself today. She sighed, knowing that she would have to talk with him about what had happened all those years ago, and she really didn't want to. Give me the words, Lord, that I need. And please, place that hedge of protection around us all.

Less than an hour later, Emma rose and tidied up the paperwork she had been working on.   Copies were sealed into envelopes that she needed to mail that day.

Abe stood in the doorway, watching her, his heart grateful that they were together again.   Emma, sensing him near, looked at him, with a puzzled frown on her face.

"You're dressed up, Abe. How come?"

He walked towards her and took her hands. "I want to spend some time with my wife, without having to worry about Charlie or any investigation.   We haven't done anything fun for weeks now, and it's time. Go. Put on your prettiest dress. I want to take you out for a meal."

Her face brightening, she turned for the stairs, then turned back.   "I have some material I need to send off today, Abe."

"Not a problem. We can do that."

Nathaniel watched as Abe and Emma headed for his vehicle, then turned to Joseph.

"Where are those two off to?" Joseph questioned.

Nathaniel shrugged. "I have no idea, but I can imagine off on a date, without us tagging along."

"I don't like that, Nathaniel."

"I don't either, but I can't say as I blame him for ditching us."

Abe settled back behind the wheel after dispatching the envelopes for Emma, and then turned to her, taking in the flowered dress she had put on and her hair loose around her face.

"Now where, Abe?"

"Where would you like to eat? I thought we'd go to a restaurant today for a meal, rather than Mac's."

"That would be nice. Thank you, sweetheart."

"And while we're eating, you can tell me where you go to fly with the eagles. I need to get you there soon, you're burning out yourself."

She nodded. "I am. I need to see my eagles."

Emma tucked her hand into the crook of Abe's elbow and let him lead her into the Italian restaurant in town. She was surprised when they were taken to a private room, but Abe just looked at her.

"This is nice, Abe."

He smiled. "It is. We need to do this, Emma, no matter what's going on. If we don't, we'll lose us."

Abe watched as his wife turned the bracelet he had given around on her wrist, a pensive look on her face.

"You're thinking hard, Emma."

She sighed and then nodded. "I am, Abe. I just want this over. I need to go see my eagles."

"Then, that's what we'll do. We'll slip away and you can tell me where to find them. How far away are they?"

"About a four-hour drive. I think if we drove it overnight, we'd be okay."

Abe tapped at Murphy's door early that evening.

"Abe, what are you doing here?" Adriel was surprised to see him. "I thought you were out on a date with your wife."

"I was. Is Murphy around?"

She shook her head. "I think he had headed for the exercise building." She stared at his face for a moment. "Is everything okay?"

Abe nodded. "It is. I just need to let Murphy know Emma and I are taking off for a few days."

"You're taking off for a few days? Just like that? How safe are you going to be?"

Abe laughed at her. "About as safe as we can be. Thanks, Adriel."

Murphy stared after Abe as he walked out of the building, then turned to Matt. "Did he really just say they're taking off for a few days?"

"That's what I heard." Matt was frustrated. "How do we keep them safe, if he does that?"

Murphy shrugged. "I guess we sit here and worry. Abe's been different the last couple of weeks."

"He has. He's chafing under the restrictions he's been facing as has Emma. I've been expecting this." Matt walked to the door. "Just make sure he can contact one of us if he needs to."

Chapter 16

Abe stood staring across the open area he could see from Emma's mountaintop. It wasn't really that high, but it was enough to make him feel closer to the heavens and to God. He drew in a deep breath, feeling himself relaxing as he did so.

Emma wrapped her arms around him from behind. "Aren't you glad we snuck away, even though the guys are upset with us?"

"It's not so much they're upset, it's that they can't provide protection for us. They're afraid we'll need it."

Emma paused, her eyes tracing the eagles' flight above her. "See, that pair? Those are the ones I've been following for a while. They are just so majestic. I'll show you their nest tomorrow."

He turned, looking down into her face, and seeing the peace and balance that had returned. "You really needed this, didn't you?"

"I did, Abe. I come out here, away from all the distractions of modern life, just spending time with God and His creation. It always made me sad I couldn't share it with you."

"And now you can." He looked around. "So, where do we set up camp?"

"There's a small cave just up the trail a little. It's about the size of a tent, just enough room for our backpacks and sleeping bags."

Sitting under the starlight later that night, Emma leaned on Abe's arm. "When I'm up here, I feel so close to God, Abe. It's like He's created this space just for me, and now us."

"I know. It's incredible." Abe still felt uneasy, feeling a sense of evil following them.

"Do you think we had a shadow?"

Abe shrugged. "I feel like we did, but I couldn't see anyone. The guys aren't happy with us, you know."

Emma nodded. "I know, but we needed to get away, Abe. We've been so close to that investigation, it's interfering in our lives. We were starting to snipe at one another, and I know that's not us."

Early morning, three days later, they packed up their gear and then stood watching as the eagles soared above them. Emma turned to Abe.

"I guess we have to go back to reality, do we?"

Abe laughed. "Unfortunately, we do. You have your court appearance next week, and we have to be away in Oak City."

Abe stopped when they were partway down the trail, a sound behind him catching his attention.

"Did you notice anyone else up here, Emma?"

She turned startled eyes on him. "No, I didn't. There's someone there, isn't there?"

"I'm afraid so. Maybe this wasn't such a good idea after all."

Emma pointed to a narrow opening. "I've gone down that way before. It's more narrow, but more sheltered. No one could see us on it."

She pulled him on to the new trail rapidly, and then pushed the bushes back into place. They waited, careful not to speak, watching.

Emma drew in a quick breath, then clapped her hands over her mouth, her eyes on Abe. He gave her a puzzled look, then stared through the branches at the two men passing by.

Emma grabbed Abe's arm and pointed down the trail they were now standing on. After traveling at a rapid pace for a while, she finally stopped.

"Talk to me, Emma. Who were they?"

"They work for Charlie and have since before I ran. He called them his general man servants, but they did a lot more than that. I always felt a sense of evil around them."

Abe nodded. "So, now we know who's after us, then. Where does this path lead and can we reach our vehicle before they do?"

"It comes out just about in the parking lot. We should be able to make it before they get there. I don't know, Abe. How did you know someone was following us?"

He shrugged as they set off again at a rapid pace. "I just thought there would be. They're covering their tracks quite well. I'm surprised they didn't try and nab us over the last few days."

"Not many people stay up on the mountains overnight.   They must have thought we went up early and came down late. I can't see them camping out. It's not their style."

As they reached the parking lot, Abe stopped Emma with a hand on her arm. "Let me check out everything first. Here, I'll take your pack and stick it in the SUV." He scanned the area as he headed for his vehicle, seeing nothing out of the ordinary. Please, Lord, let us get home safely.

He tucked Emma into the vehicle and pulled away, still not seeing the men. Emma watched his face.

"What did you do, Abe?"

He smiled. "What do you mean, what did I do?"

"You've done something."

He laughed, finally admitting he had. "I found out which vehicle was theirs and took a page out of Deirdre's book." He handed her two valve caps. "They'll not be after us for a while. Pull out your map and plot us a way home that's longer but through more towns."

"Frankie's Deirdre did that?"

Abe laughed even harder. "You've never heard their story, have you? When they had their adventure, Deirdre pulled the valve caps off eight tires from their kidnappers and took them with her."

"I would never have expected that from her."

"She's scary, but you're scarier."

She smacked his arm. "Behave yourself, Abe. I'm not that scary."

"No, with you, it's your mind that's scary. We can't keep up with how you think and process facts."

She nodded. "I'm always been like that. Dad was too. That's why he set up the computer programming company he had. Auntie Em shut it down when he died."

"That's where you got your program from, isn't it? You kept that one program."

She turned her gray eyes on him. "You're the only one who has ever figured that out."

"Not even Jace?"

She shook her head. "Not that I know of. I've kept that very private."

"That you have." Abe's eyes moved to the rearview mirror. "We're almost home, sweetheart. You're looking more like yourself."

"Thank you, Abe. It was definitely worth the risk we took. I hope your guys aren't too upset with us."

"We're not the first ones to run. Ian usually is offering his services to help the ladies run."

Murphy walked towards Abe later that day. He and Adriel had been away when Abe and Emma returned home.

"How was your trip?"

Abe turned towards Murphy. "It was good. We needed it, but more than that, Emma needed it. She was starting to burn out with all the work she's been putting in."

Murphy nodded. "The guys figured it was something like that. You had us worried, though. You never said anything about where you were heading."

Abe stared at Murphy. Then, his eyes slid closed. "I didn't, did I? All I was thinking about was getting Emma away for a few days."

Murphy pointed at Abe. "That right there says it all. You need to step back as leader in this, Abe, and let us take over. You're not thinking of the consequences."

"Right, just like you all did?"

Murphy stared at him, then started to laugh. "Guilty! So from now on, I'm in charge of you two and your security, and you'll just have to take what we dish out. It's our turn."

"I can tell you Emma's going to fight you on it."

"Make sure she doesn't. It may mean your life or hers." Murphy walked away as Abe's eyes followed him.

Abe was torn. He needed to talk to Emma again, but he had work to do in the business office. Finally, he turned back to the house, looking for Emma.

Emma slipped her matching navy suit jacket over her white shell and navy skirt and then into her low-heeled pumps, dressed for a day in court. She hated being in the open like that, having to defend and justify her findings. No one ever really understood how she searched out her material.

Abe turned as she approached. "Ready to go?"

She nodded, then looked at him with a question in her eyes. "Aren't you heading for Oak City today?"

He shook his head. "We don't need the whole team, so Nathaniel staying with us."

She looked around him at Nathaniel, then back at him. "It's going to be a very boring day for you."

"Not likely." He turned to Nathaniel. "Ready to go?"

Nathaniel nodded. "We are. Caleb sent out some off-duty officers for security as well."

Emma stopped in her walk and spun around. "Now, tell me, how many of you are there?"

Nathaniel laughed at the look on her face. "Hopefully, enough to keep you and Abe alive. We have no idea when or where he will strike again."

"I think he'll strike again soon." Abe followed Emma into the backseat of the SUV. He nodded to the officer in the front passenger seat, recognizing his face but not able to place his name.

Emma looked around, then caught sight of the officer in the front. "Bill, how are you? And your family?"

The officer turned, answering her questions, as Abe looked between the two of them. *Lord, I don't know how she does it, but please, dear Lord, protect us today. I can feel the evil closing in.*

Emma sat impassively in the witness box, answering the questions asked her by the prosecutor. She was not looking forward to when it became the defense attorney's turn.

She had had a time with him the last trial she had testified at.

The defense attorney approached her, papers in his hand.

"Miss Donovan, may I ask you how you arrived at your conclusions?"

"I'm sorry, but it's Mrs. Finlay." She stared at him, knowing he was well aware of that fact.

"I don't see where a name change has come through."

"Your Honour, the name change is there. It has been there for years. It is not acceptable to me for the attorney to completely ignore that fact." Emma appealed to the judge.

"You're correct, Mrs. Finlay. Mr. Lee, you have the correct name to address her by. Ensure you do. I will not accept any of your normal tactics today."

Flustered, the attorney returned to his table, speaking with his client. He finally turned to the judge and indicated he had no questions.

Dismissed, Emma walked back to sit with Abe. Abe caught her hand in his and then listened to the rest of the testimony from the morning. The prosecutor approached Emma at the end of the morning session.

"I don't know what you did, Emma, but he backed off so quickly. That's very unusual for him."

"I think he had a plan in place and wanted to trip me up on my name somewhere down the line in his questioning. He didn't get an opportunity to do so, thanks to the judge."

He nodded. "You're all finished now. Thank you for your time and effort."

She blinked. "That's it? I'm finished?"

He laughed. "You are. Now, go enjoy the rest of your day with Abe."

Nathaniel was standing behind them and pointed at the door the judge had used.

"We can't go out that way, Nathaniel," Emma protested.

"We can and we will. I spoke with the judge this morning before the trial started. It's a safer way to get you out of here."

Nathaniel stopped them at the bottom of the stairs to the garage. Something was off, he could feel it.

"Bill, wait here with them. I'm going for the vehicle." Nathaniel scanned the area around him, as he heard gunfire from the parking lot above. Quickening his steps into a run, he slid behind the wheel and pulled out to head for them.

Gunfire could be heard in the parking garage as he stopped. Bill almost shoved both Abe and Emma into the vehicle, then jump in behind them, slamming the door as bullets hit the vehicle. Nathaniel hit the accelerator, heading for the ramp to the surface.

Abe sat, back against the door, huddled on the floor, Emma in his arms. Bill's head was barely above the door edge, searching for the gunmen.

Nathaniel slammed on the brakes as he saw the cruisers waiting at the entrance and then Jake running towards him. He lowered his window enough he could talk with him.

"Nathaniel, go. They'll let you through. Is everyone all right?"

Bill went to speak, then stopped. "Emma's been hit. We need an escort if we can Jake."

Jake shot Nathaniel a quick glance, then ran for the cruisers. One pulled out and headed towards the hospital as Nathaniel pulled in behind it. Bill reached for the first aid kit and grabbing bandages, shoved them at Abe. Abe took a look at Bill, then down at Emma, pushing the bandages against the wound on the side of her head.

"How'd that happen, Bill?" Abe was confused. "I thought we were in before the gunfire got close to us."

"There was more than one shooter, I think, Abe. He nailed Emma as she was getting in. Somewhere in your vehicle is a bullet."

Abe's heart sank as he watched the blood soak into the gauze. Please, Lord, protect her. Save her.

John Thompson slid into the vehicle and assessed Emma. He turned and said something to the waiting nurse.

"Abe. We need you to let go of Emma. I want to slide her this way and then we can get her assessed. Abe?" John shared a look with Nathaniel.

Nathaniel turned in his seat. "Abe." He reached and shook his shoulder.

Abe looked up, shock evident in his face. "Nathaniel?"

"Abe, let John have Emma. He needs to get her inside."

Abe nodded and loosened his grasp on Emma, his tortured eyes following as she was moved to a stretcher and then inside. Bill hurried him in and to a room where he would be secure.

Nathaniel approached the room slowly, his eyes following the stretchers being rushed into the department. He had heard there had been a number of officers shot. He turned as Eddie walked towards him, his steps heavy and sorrow on his face.

"Nathaniel, how's Emma?"

"I haven't heard yet, Eddie. What happened over there?"

Eddie shook his head. "We'll be sorting that out for quite a while. We got a call about an active shooter. We had officers escorting a prisoner in and they were shot as was their prisoner." He too turned to watch the commotion going on. "Caleb was there and got hit."

"Caleb? How is he?"

"I haven't heard. We have at least one officer dead as well as the prisoner." He nodded towards the room Nathaniel had been walking towards. "We think that the ones after Emma and Abe took advantage of what was going on in the parking lot."

Abe looked up as his uncle and Nathaniel entered.

"Eddie?" His voice a question, Abe walked towards him. "What's going on?"

Eddie paused, then told Abe what he had told Nathaniel. Abe sank back against the wall as he heard about Caleb.

"I don't think Caleb has ever been hurt on duty, other than the odd bump or scrape."

Eddie shook his head. "He hasn't. I can't stay, Abe. I need to get back to the courthouse, but I wanted to check on you two and let you know what had happened."

Abe watched his uncle walk away, shoulders stooped with the burden of the day. His eyes sought Nathaniel's.

"There were more than just Caleb."

Nathaniel nodded, his eyes on Bill. "Bill, if you want to go find out what's happened, you can."

Bill shook his head. "No, I was asked to provide security for you and I will. We need to get someone with Emma. And I guess that would be me right at the moment."

He walked past them, shooting glances at the gathering crowd in the waiting room.

John Thompson stood, staring at the X-Ray he had taken of Emma. No bleeding on the brain, no fracture, he thought. That's good. Then he turned to the blood work and paused, taking a look at Emma and then back at the blood work. He needed to talk with Abe.

"Sue, can you have Abe Finlay brought here?"

She nodded and headed to find Abe. Abe pushed the door open slowly, his eyes searching for Emma. Pausing at her bedside, he touched her face and then reached for her hand, stopping when he saw the blood on his own hand.

John saw the hesitation and the reason why and pulled Abe aside to help him clean up.

"How is she, John?" Abe's voice was quiet and tight.

"She's a very lucky lady, Abe. No bleeding to the brain, no fracture. She will have a scar there, though. Right now, she's still unconscious and I'll be moving her to a room she can be monitored in." He stopped, then looked at Abe, not quite sure how to proceed. "I ran blood work on her, Abe. Tell me, have you two talked about children?"

Abe's eyes shot to John's. "Not really. Why?" At the look on the physician's face, Abe's eyes slid closed. "You're telling me we'll be adding to our family, are you?"

"I am. She'll need to see her own doctor as soon as she can."

Abe's eyes sought his wife. "She has never said, John, but when she was so sick years ago, I think she lost a baby."

John's hand came down on Abe's shoulder as he lifted the young couple up in prayer. "I can see how she would have difficulty telling you, with all you've gone through. I can't tell you what to do now, but she needs to rest and she needs to keep the stress down."

Abe gave a snort of laughter at that. "That won't happen, John, as long as Charlie is still on the loose. Today was just an example of how far he'll go."

John shook his head, then looked at Emma as she began to stir. "I'll leave you two for now, but Sue will be back when they're ready with a room for her."

John walked away, heading for Caleb's bedside. Caleb was awake, the vest having taken most of the shock of the bullets. He stared at his upper arm where he had been grazed as he turned, then looked up at John's face.

"How're Abe and Emma?"

"Emma was hit but she'll be fine. Now, about you."

Abe watched as Emma's head turned on the pillow, willing her awake. She stilled again and this time he thought she slept. He reached for her hand, noting it to be cold, and trying to warm it. He reached over and tucked her other hand under the blanket, then turned as Sue entered the room.

"It will be about an hour or more before we move her, Abe. We'll try and keep the noise and commotion down as much as we can for you, but it's a very busy department right now."

Abe nodded. "If you see Nathaniel, send him in, will you? Thanks. Bill, I think, needs to go be with his fellow officers."

Sue looked up at a tap at the door. Don Woods poked his head in.

"Abe, can I talk to you for a moment?"

Abe gave a reluctant look at his wife, then moved to the hallway to speak with Don.

"We heard what happened, and that your guys are in Oak City. Murphy called. They're on their way home in about six hours, but he asked if we could step in for them."

Abe reached to shake his hand. "Thank you, Don. It seems the balance is more on my side than yours."

Don shrugged. "Not the way I see it. How's Emma?"

"She was grazed by the bullet, but John says everything looks good. She'll be moved to a room soon."

Don nodded. "We'll be here outside her door. Let us know if we can get you anything."

Chapter 17

Emma's hand went to her head, the IV pulling on her arm. Slowly, her eyes opened, and she looked around through blurry vision. Where was she? Her head hurt so much, she thought, then closed her eyes again.

Abe watched as Emma roused and reached for her hand. Emma lay still but her hand closed on Abe's. It was hours after the incident.

"Abe, what happened?" Eyes squinting against the light, Emma watched her husband.

"Somehow as we were getting in the vehicle, you got hit with a bullet. Right here." He pointed to his own head. "John's seen you and said you'll be fine, other than a headache for a few days."

"Only a headache? I can see more than that in your eyes."

Abe nodded, not sure how to tell her. "There was a shooting in the parking lot.

Caleb was grazed by a bullet, but they have three other officers wounded and an officer dead, as well as a prisoner."

Emma's eyes slid closed as she prayed. Then her eyes popped open and she stared at Abe.

"That's not everything, Mr. Finlay. I can see it in your eyes and your face."

Abe studied his wife, then leaned close. "John did some blood work while you were in Emergency. Is there something you want to tell me?"

She went to shake her head and stopped at the pain. "Not that I know of. Why are you so mysterious? What blood work did John run?"

"Because of your age, he ran a certain test, just in case he needed to send you to surgery."

Dawning comprehension on her face, Emma's hand went to her mouth. "No, this isn't a good time, Abe. I can't be."

"Whether it's a good time or not, you are."

Tears flooded her eyes and she turned from him.

"Emma, I figured it out. I know what you wanted to tell me." Her head turned back to him and he saw the shimmer of tears. Clearing his throat, he continued, "I have a good idea of what it was. Oh, sweetheart, I wish I could have been there with you."

Tears flowing down her cheeks, Emma nodded. "The doctors tried everything they could, Abe, but they couldn't save the little one. There had been too much stress, I was too sick, and whatever drugs he used affected it." She reached to wipe the tears from his face. "I didn't want you going after him in revenge for that."

Abe watched as tears flowed down his wife's face, then reached to lower the bedrail. Laying down beside her, he pulled her into his arms and held her, his tears mingling with her. Exhausted, they both slept.

Anna, the nurse on the floor, stopped as she opened the door, then shook her head. She found a blanket and covered Abe and then pulled up the bedrail. She did her check on Emma, then walked out, turning off the overhead light, just leaving the light at the head of the bed on.

John Thompson stopped her as she exited the room.

"How's Emma?"

She smiled. "They're both asleep. Emma's been awake by the looks of it."

John nodded. "Then I won't go in. I'll stop in tomorrow morning before I leave."

He turned to walk back to the Emergency Department, heart heavy with what had happened that day. Why, Lord? Why did it have to happen? And why did it have to be Sue who got caught in the crossfire?

He crossed to the elevator and took it to the ICU unit. Nodding to the nurse, he headed for Sue's room. Standing he watched as she fought to survive. Please, Lord, heal her. We need this lady.

Murphy stood in the doorway of Emma's room the next morning, then shot a look back down the hall. All of Abe's guys were there as were their ladies. Don had stayed through the night and was now on his way home.

He walked on quiet feet to the bedside, shaking his head at the two. Touching Abe's shoulder, he awakened him.

Abe turned, eyes blurry from sleep. "Murphy? What time is it?"

"It's about 6 in the morning, Abe. Did you get any sleep?'

Abe nodded, then tried to figure out how to work the bedrail. Murphy lowered it for him, and Abe sat, then turned to look back at Emma.

"How's Emma?"

"She's got a headache and will have to take it easy for a couple of weeks. That's going to be hard once she starts feeling better." He searched Murphy's face. "Talk to me, Murphy."

Murphy's eyes rose to stare at the wall. "Sue was one of the officers hit. They're not sure if she'll survive."

Abe's heart raised in prayer for his friend. He knew Murphy and Sue had been friends for years. "What else?"

"Caleb's been discharged. The other two officers will be by tomorrow." Murphy stared at Abe. "We found the bullet in the SUV, Abe. It just missed Nathaniel. It was buried in the back of his seat."

Abe's eyes slid closed at that. So close, Lord. Thank you for your protection.

"I gather the team's out there?"

Murphy nodded. "And their ladies. They wouldn't stay away." He turned to the door. "You need to come speak with them.

Rebecca and Gideon are on their way in as well. They didn't get home until about 3 this morning."

Abe rose, then turned to look at Emma. Then he shook his head and followed Murphy out to the waiting room.

The men stood as they saw Abe approaching them.

"How's Emma?" Matt searched Abe's face.

"She's still sleeping but John said she'll have a headache for a few days." Abe's eyes roamed the faces of his men and then their wives, turning to Gideon. They stopped when he saw the look on his sister's face. "Rebecca?"

She threw herself into her brother's arms. "I was so afraid, Abe, when I heard about the shooting. I'm so thankful Emma's okay."

Abe hugged his sister, his eyes going to her husband. Silent communication went between the two men.

"Thanks to you all. Murphy, you're in charge for now. I need to spend the time with Emma." He turned and walked back to his wife's room.

Eyes turned to Murphy as he watched his friend and business partner walk away, his heart heavy at what he knew was coming.

"So, where do we go from here, Murphy?" Ian's quiet voice broke through the silence.

Murphy turned, lost in thought. "It's going to be a tough one, guys. Once Emma starts to feel better, Abe's going to want to be more involved, and we can't let him. Once we have them home today, I suggest we meet and come up with some plans." He sought out Nathaniel, watching his face, trying to assess his thoughts.

Nathaniel approached Murphy as the others were leaving. "I'm staying with you, Murphy. So is Luke. It was too close for all of us yesterday."

"That it was, Nathaniel. God had his hand on us for sure."

Abe approached the two men as they stood talking and making plans.

"Murphy, Emma's got her discharge. How do you want to handle getting her downstairs to the vehicle?"

Murphy turned to study the hospital corridor, then walked towards an exit. As he came back, his eyes watched a woman standing in the waiting room, looking around.

"Abe, Nathaniel." As they approached him, he nodded at the waiting room. "Somehow, I don't think she's here for a family member or friend. Abe, can you get Emma ready?" He handed Abe a bag. "Rebecca bought her some clothes that would be easier for her to wear."

When Abe had left, Murphy turned to Nathaniel. "I don't like this, Nathaniel. There's really no good way of getting them to the parking lot or even to the entrance."

Nathaniel nodded. "I know. There's not a lot of activity, though."

Murphy agreed. "That could work in our favour or not."

Chapter 18

Abe walked heavily down the back stairs of his home to the kitchen. He needed food and drink, but his heart was upstairs with his wife. She had roused enough for them to get her home and for him to tuck her into bed, then she had slept. He had been warned this would happen and that he needed to wake her every couple of hours for the first day or so.

Hearing a tap at the front door and then it opening, he headed for the coffee pot. Murphy had called a team meeting and wanted Abe there for his input.

Matt watched as Abe moved slowly around the kitchen and the living room. Something more than just what had happened the day before was going on, he thought. Please, Lord, be with these two. They need Your protection.

Murphy looked up from some notes he had been making. "Abe, where do we stand with trainees coming in or our doing security?"

Abe brought his mind back to business and narrowed his eyes as he thought through the next few weeks. "We have a team of five in for four days next week, then a team of six the following week for five days." He paused, his mind searching for what he could remember of the contracts. "Then, we have a break for a week, and back at it the following week with a team of four."

"What about Emma's work?"

Abe shrugged. "She keeps it pretty close to herself. Whatever she has been working on, I think she said was good, that she was waiting for some more data to come in. Jace can pick up a lot of that, and Naomi has been working at home as well." He sighed. "She's going to want to be back at it as soon as she can."

"Don't let her, Abe. She needs to rest." Matt glanced towards the stairway. "If she doesn't, she'll end up sicker than she should be."

"We need to make some decisions, Abe, that I know already you won't like." Murphy watched his friend's face and saw the acceptance there. "How do we keep you two safe?"

Abe shrugged. "They've already proven they can and will use any opportunity to try and get to us. I guess taking their valve caps really didn't slow them down that much."

The men laughed at that, then Ian spoke. "Emma's not going to like not having her freedom, but it may come to the point where we'll have to stash you two somewhere."

Abe stood and stared pacing. "I know, Ian. I know. I just don't know how we'd do that though."

"We'll figure it out. Jake was out earlier today. He's making progress and has tracked down some addresses where he thinks Charlie has been staying. Charlie's keeping under the radar."

Abe looked to the kitchen as he heard Emma's phone chime, a frown on his face. "Just a minute, let me grab Emma's phone."

His face paled as he read the message. Charlie was determined to get to Emma.

"Abe?" Micah spoke from behind him.

Abe turned, handing him the phone. "It's just gotten worse, guys. Charlie's making more and new threats. Micah, can you send that on to Jake, please?"

"What did it say, Abe?" Joseph exchange glances with the other men.

"Just that he knows where she lives, where she works, and when she's not there. And that he was coming for her."

"Still vague, but enough that we need to take the precautions we've been discussing." Murphy watched Abe's face. "What are you thinking, Abe?"

"That I want this over with now. How do we draw him out without putting Emma at any more risk than she is?"

"She's the only one that can do that, Abe, unfortunately." Murphy had thought it through as much as he could.

Abe nodded, then sighed. "I know, I know. I just wish there was some way we could get to him."

Charlie stood watching the house, then looked at the two men standing with him. "What happened? You told me you shot her?"

The older of the two men shrugged. "We did. But we couldn't get a clear shot, not with the angle we were working from."

"Fix your mistake. Instead of killing her, bring her to me. I want to see her suffer."

The younger man narrowed his eyes and hid his shudder. This was getting out of hand, he thought. He hadn't signed on to murder or assault. He followed the other two men back to the vehicle. He had a decision to make. So far, he hadn't been involved in anything more than being an onlooker.

The men separated, Charlie heading for the rundown apartment he had rented under an assumed name, the older of the two other men for the local bar. The younger man hesitated, looked around, then made his decision. He headed for the police department, wanting to speak with someone.

Jake Wilson looked up from his desk at a knock. Eddie stood there.

"There's someone wanting to talk to you about Emma and Abe. We've put him into an interrogation room."

"What about?"

"He didn't say, just that he knew what Charlie was up to."

Jake sighed, then rose. "Come with me, Eddie. I can use your help on this. It would be nice if it was a break in the case."

"That it would be."

Jake studied the man seated across from him. "What made you decide to come in?"

The younger man, having given his name as Carl, shrugged. "I can't stomach what he's planning. I'm just new to his men, and I wouldn't have even hired on if I knew what he was like."

"So, walk us through what you know about what he's done in the past and what he's planning." Jake was direct in his words.

"I can tell you it's not good for that lady." Carl was nervous, shifting in his chair, twisting his hands. He lifted his eyes to Jake and then to Eddie. "He wants her brought to him and he wants to make her suffer. I can't let that happen."

Jake stood outside Abe's door later that day, waiting for Abe to answer. He turned as the door opened and was shocked at the devastation and fatigue he saw in Abe's face.

"Abe?"

"Come on in, Jake. Emma's laying down in the living room, but she's drowsy."

"Thanks, Abe." He laid a hand on Abe's arm. "Are you okay?"

Abe stopped, then shook his head. "I've some things to work through that are hard. That doesn't include this. What brings you out?"

"I need to talk to you and Emma, if she's awake."

"Let me call Murphy in. He's taking over our security for now."

Murphy slowly sat, watching the look on Jake's face. The news wouldn't be good. He shot a look at Abe, sitting on the couch, arm around Emma. Emma was cuddled up to her husband, eyes closed as she drowsed.

"What brings you out here, Jake?" Murphy repeated the question Abe had asked earlier.

"Frankly, I'm not sure where to start. Charlie and his men have been up in the rocks behind you again, Abe, as late as about five hours ago. One of his newest hires has decided he doesn't like Charlie's way of doing business and came and talked to Eddie and me.

"He is adamant that Charlie is determined to get his hands on Emma and make her suffer."

"We get that, Jake, but what makes this fellow so different?"

"He's young, he's been with Charlie's men for a few weeks now. He's able to provide information and addresses that we didn't have. I have our team working through it. Frankie's back on Monday and is heading in to that search as well.

"What do we do, though, with you two?"

Murphy spoke. "That's what we've been trying to plan, Jake. It's hard, though, when we have no idea when Charlie will be in the hills or even around Emma. Abe and Emma have both mentioned in the past the feeling of evil they've sensed when they're out and about."

Jake nodded. "I get that, too, Murphy." He blew out a breath of frustration. "I can feel him closing in on you two, Abe, but I have no idea what to do with you."

Abe laughed, his movement causing Emma's eyes to open. "We don't either. Murphy and the guys are working on it, but they're not sure what to do either."

"We go on the offensive, Jake. That's what we do." Emma peered through pain-filled eyes at him. "We chase him down. Go to the media. Flood the area with flyers. I make a stand where he can get at me."

Abe shook his head at the last one. "Not happening, Emma."

She looked up at him. "At some point, it will, Abe, and there's nothing we can do to stop it. He's got to be stopped. Unless he's found and transported away to face murder charges somewhere else, I'll have to face him down."

"So, how do we do that then, Emma, and keep you safe?"

"Have your PR people put out a statement on our behalf, giving as many of the details you can without compromising any investigation. I have the information back now on my aunt. It was murder, plain and simple. Use that. He thought he could get away with that, and I would like to see him up on charges for that."

Jake nodded. "We can do that. The media are clamouring for more information about what happened to you two."

Murphy spoke up. "Just be very careful, Jake. This man is a loose cannon, a time bomb waiting to go off."

Jake agreed. "I'll have a statement prepared, then have someone bring it out for you to look over, hopefully by tomorrow."

Abe nodded as he felt Emma once more relax against him. "That means we'll be more of a target, Murphy."

Murphy nodded. "I know. Let me talk to the guys and see what we can do. The only option is for you two to live in the safe room for now."

Abe started laughing. "Emma has made her feelings quite clear on that one, I think, Murphy."

Emma stirred from where she had been laying on the couch later that evening. Abe was asleep in his chair across from her, she saw. Sitting up, she reached for Meow Too who had been cuddled up beside her.

"Have you had your food, my girl? Let's go see."

Emma headed for the kitchen, stopping to make sure the doors were locked. She stopped at the fridge, and holding Meow Too in one hand, opened it to find something for herself. She reached for a bottle of juice and then froze. What was this in the fridge? She stifled a scream, then turned to find Abe.

She shook him. "Abe! Please wake up."

Instantly alert, Abe was on his feet. "Emma, what are you doing up?"

"I was going to make sure the kitten had food but stopped to grab a bottle of juice. He's been in the house, Abe. He's been in our home!"

"How do you know?" Abe was concerned at the ashen look on her face.

"Check the fridge! He's been in here!"

Abe froze at her words, then strode past her to the fridge. Eyes sliding closed, he reached for his phone to call Jake. He would not be happy to hear this.

Chapter 19

Grim faces greeted Jake as he walked into Abe's home. His heart sinking, he realized how dangerous this man was.

"What did you find, Abe?"

Abe turned hard angry eyes on him. "Emma opened the fridge and found this." Abe pointed at the open door.

A picture of Abe and Emma coming down the mountain was leaning against the milk carton. Both of their faces were crossed off in red.

"How did he get in here?"

"Joseph's working on that. That picture was taken just a few days ago. We were up on that mountain to get away. They followed us down until we took a different path. They were that close, Jake." Abe was angrier than he had ever been in his life, and was working on cooling down his temper. Lord, I need to stay calm and focused, but it's so hard. Take over, please.

Jake looked at each of the men standing in the kitchen. Abe's full team was there. He could see Emma on the couch in the living room, the kitten wrapped in her arms, as she lay, her eyes closed, with tear traces on her face.

Jake nodded. "There's no point in the crime scene team coming out. How do you think he got in?"

Nathaniel spoke up. "We've had some odd blips with the security tape and Abe's security log. Somehow, he's figured out how to get around them."

"I'm working on changes to that, Jake, but we need to find this man." Joseph bit the words off as he spoke.

Charlie paced the small rundown room he had rented, or sort of rented. He was almost broke. His men didn't know that they weren't going to get paid. People were after him from both sides of the law, and he was getting ready to run.

The flickering television caught his attention, and he moved to turn up the sounds.

"Public relations personnel from our police department are appealing for the public's help in finding this man." Charlie stared as his picture appeared on the screen.

"We have been advised that he is considered armed and dangerous and that the public should not approach him.

"Officer Whyte, you are with the public relations branch of our police. What more can you tell us?"

"Thank you, Peter. We are seeking to apprehend this gentleman, Charles West, on behalf of our department and numerous other police services. He is wanted on a number of charges of murder, assault, bank fraud.

"Our police service is looking for him on a warrant of attempted murder and assault as well as stalking and harassment. Please contact our tip line if you see him."

"May I ask if this is related to the incident at the courthouse?"

The officer looked at Peter, then directly back at the camera. "It is, Peter. During that incident at the courthouse, we believe men hired by him attempted to murder a well-known member of our community and his wife, Abe and Emma Finlay. They have both agreed to go public with this knowledge, hoping that someone will see him and contact us. Thank you."

Charles stared at the screen, then the bottle in his hand flew at the television, shattering it. Now, what, he thought, as he stormed around the round, his hands running through his sparse hair.

He turned, leaving the room. He knew what he needed. He just had to find it.

Emma snuggled down into Abe's arm as they sat on the couch. He flicked off the television and stared into space.

"Do you think it will work, Abe?" Emma's hesitant voice was not like herself.

He shook his head to clear it, then looked down at the russet head resting on his shoulder. "I pray it does, Emma, and that what's happening will be over. I don't want you hurt again."

She sighed. "Somehow, I don't think it is, Abe. I really don't think so. They haven't found the sniper yet. From what I could find on her, she'll never give up until we're dead or she is."

Abe's movements stilled as his heart race faster. "I know, sweetheart. Jake's doing everything he can to find her. I pray he does."

Emma nodded, then yawned. "I pray he does to, but I don't think he will. She's hidden too well. That's the problem. Women can hide and be in plain sight."

"Lydia mentioned something like that one time too." He looked down at Emma, then at the clock. It was still early but he could tell she was tired. "How be we get you up to bed?"

She nodded. "Abe, I'm sorry I couldn't tell you."

Abe hugged her, then standing, swung her up in his arms. "That's not an issue, sweetheart. We've discussed it and I consider it past. We've had to deal with it, grieve, but now we move on."

Ginny Smothers looked at the man sitting across from her. "You want me to do what?"

"I need them dead now." Charlie was adamant on that.

"I told you when you found me, and you hired me I did it in my time and my way. Unless you have a couple of extra million you want to throw my way."

He stared at her, then abruptly stood. "I hired you to get rid of them within a certain timeframe. I would say that timeframe is past."

She shook her head. "No, you hired me to kill them. There was no time frame involved then, but there sounds like there is now. If that is the case, cough up the extra money.”

He stared at her with hate, and then walked away. His two men followed him. She watched him walk away, and then rose herself and headed for the back door. She never went in and out the front door if she could help it.

Bill Walton stared at the front door and then the back. He stood, hesitant as to which one to follow, and then followed Charlie. He watched as he headed for a vehicle and then drove away. Bill walked around to the back of the restaurant, but as he thought, the woman was gone. Now what, he thought, as he headed for the department building, hoping to find Jake or Eddie.

Neither Jake or Eddie were in the building, but he ran in to Frankie.

“Frankie, do you know where Jake or Eddie are?”

Frankie, looking rested and relaxed, turned. “No, I don’t, Bill. I can reach one of them for you, if you need. Come into my office.”

“I really should speak with Jake. I just saw Charlie West meeting with a woman, and

I didn't like what I was hearing in their conversation."

Frankie's hand froze as he finished dialing Jake's number. "Were they discussing Abe and Emma?"

Bill shrugged. "I think so, but they never said names."

"Jake? Frankie. Yes, it was good to be away. I need to apologize to you. Thanks. Listen, I have Bill Walton here. He needs to speak with you. He has some information on Charlie and his sniper." Frankie's eyes steadied on Bill. "Sure, we can meet you there.

"Jake asked if we could meet at Mac's. He's heading there to grab a meal."

Bill shrugged. "Works for me if you've the time."

"I do. I've heard what's been going on since Deirdre and I were away. I want this to end for Abe's sake."

Seated at a booth in the back of the cafe, the three men exchanged idle talk until Mac placed their orders in front of them. Mac didn't walk away right away. Instead, he studied each of the men, then handed Jake a letter.

"This was left for whoever the investigating detective is. I understand it's you, Jake. I have no idea who left it. It just appeared on our counter tonight."

Jake frowned as he took the letter, then shared a glance with both Frankie and Bill.

"Thanks, Mac." Using his knife, he slit the enveloped and pulled out the single page of notepaper. Unfolding it, he read it, then shot a glance at Frankie.

"Now, this is interesting." He handed the note to Frankie.

Frankie hesitated before taking it. "Are you sure, Jake?"

"You're part of the team working this, Frankie. I could use your thoughts. Then, we're going to have to find Caleb." He turned to Bill. "What was it you had for me?"

Bill described what he had witnessed, Jake listening intently as was Frankie.

"Can you describe her enough to get a sketch for us?"

Bill nodded. "I think I can, but I know I've seen her somewhere and not as a sniper."

Jake and Frankie exchanged glances. "Really? Where?"

Bill shook his head. "I can't place her at the moment, but I know I will."

Jake had his phone out and was sending a text message off to Jace. "Did you hear a name?" Bill supplied it to Jake. "Jace will work on tracking that down. We can't go to Emma right now, and I wish I could."

"Try Micah's Kat. She might help." Frankie spoke up.

"That she may. Do you want to ask her, you know her better than I do?"

Frankie agreed. "Now about this letter. It's strange."

"I know it." Jake reached to take a photo of it. "I'm going to have to go see Abe in the morning. I just wish this was all over with."

Frankie and Bill agreed. Bill's attention then wandered through the cafe and his glance stopped on two men sitting near the front of the building. "That's them, fellows. Those are the two men I saw with Charlie."

Jake reached for his phone. Now was the time to move in. "If we can get these fellows, then just maybe we can get to Charlie."

"What do we charge them with?" Bill was curious.

"For starters, they're known associates of a murderer. I'm sure we find lots on them when we run their prints. If they've been with him, they're involved in what he has been involved in." Frankie watched the two men, noting they had just received their meal. "At least the cafe isn't too busy right at the moment."

Frankie moved to stand. "I need to let Mac know what's coming. He'll need to warn his staff."

Jake nodded. "You know Mac much better than I do, Frankie. Go ahead."

Bill watched as unmarked and marked cruisers pulled into the lot and saw the reaction of the two men. They stood, looking for another entrance. Jake nodded and he and Bill walked towards them, with Frankie coming from the kitchen area.

"Going somewhere?" Frankie's voice caused the two men to spin and stare at him.

"Yeah, we remembered we needed to be somewhere."

"Actually, you're needing to come with us."

"What for?" The belligerent response came from the younger of the two.

"Well, let's see. Attempted murder, assault, harassment. That's just for starters." Jake nodded at the officers who had entered.

Watching the men taken away, Jake turned with a sigh. "I guess that means I don't get my meal."

Frankie started to laugh as Mac headed Jake his meal in a takeout box, a grin on his face.

"Of course you do, Jake. Come back tomorrow and I'll have something hot and fresh for you."

Jake shook his head at Mac's words. "I'm not sure it will be tomorrow, Mac, but soon."

"Frankie, can you do me a favour?" Jake stopped by Frankie's side. "Can you head out to Abe's and let him know what's up?" Jake held up the letter. "He needs to know about this yesterday."

"Let me get a picture of it, okay. Then, I will. I just hope Emma's still talking to me."

Jake stared at Frankie. "You weren't here. Did you hear about the shooting at the courthouse?"

Frankie nodded. "But I don't see what that has to do with Emma."

Jake's eyes slid closed as he realized a mistake had been made. "Frankie, you're still on the investigation and just back this afternoon. When we had that shooting at the courthouse, Emma had been in court that day. We figure those two we just arrested took advantage of the shooting and tried to kill Abe and Emma. Emma was grazed by the bullet."

Frankie's eyes shot to Jake's. "That's the first I've heard this." Anger briefly flickered across his face. "Not your fault, Jake. You've been fair about this, and I haven't had a chance to get up to speed on what has happened around here. I haven't spoken with Abe at all since I got back late last night."

"Emma's fine, thankfully. Head out there, will you? I'll catch up with you in a bit."

Chapter 20

Frankie hesitated before knocking on Abe's door. He wasn't sure any more what his reception would be. He stepped back to the edge of the porch and scanned the area the best he could in the growing dusk, the scent of the roses and honeysuckle Emma had planted heavy in the air.

"Frankie? What brings you out here at this time of night? You and not Jake?" Abe was puzzled.

"Abe, Jake asked me to come see you and Emma." He stepped into the entryway and looked around. "How is Emma?"

"She's doing better every day, getting anxious to get back to work. Come on, we're in the office. Can I get you a coffee or something?"

"Coffee sounds great. I didn't get to finish my meal at Mac's."

Abe turned. "Then, you haven't had your meal?" When Frankie shook his head,

Abe continued, "Come, I'll get you some of the casserole Emma made today. You can eat while we talk."

Frankie hesitated once again as he entered Abe's home office. Emma was stretched out on the couch, reading, with Meow Too on top of her. She looked up as Frankie entered.

"Frankie. How nice to see you! Did you and Deirdre have a nice vacation?" Her greeting put Frankie at ease as he sat.

"We did, thank you, Emma. And I hear you've been having an adventure? How are you feeling?"

She snorted, startling the kitten, who shot off her and then up onto Frankie's lap, almost into his plate of food. Emma giggled at that. "I'm getting there, Frankie. The headaches are much better." She swung her feet to the floor as Abe headed her a cup of tea and then sat beside her. "Eat, then you can tell us why you're here."

Frankie set his plate down on the table and searched the faces of the couple sitting across from him. "Jake asked me to come out and talk to you. There have been some developments that he's deep into, just from tonight."

"What developments would they have been?" Abe watched his friend's face, trying to gauge what was coming.

"For starters, we've arrested two of the men with Charlie. Of all place, Jake, Bill and I were in Mac's for a meal and they came in. Secondly, Mac found a letter addressed to the head investigator in your case left on the counter in his cafe." Frankie pulled out his phone. "It is really strange. But before I show you the letter, I should also tell you that Bill Walton was in a restaurant, not recognizing that Charlie was there until he heard a bit of his conversation. He was meeting with the hit woman, of all things."

Emma and Abe shared a glance, then Emma spoke without taking her eyes off Abe. "He's getting careless, Frankie. He always does before he moves on. From what I can see, though, his finances are gone. That's why he was so desperate to get my trust funds. The authorities have been able to track his money trail and seized the funds." She turned back to study Frankie. "Is Jake aware of that?"

Frankie shook his head. "I'm not sure. I just got back into the office this afternoon." He stared down at his phone, then looked at Abe. "Here, read this letter. Then talk to me."

Abe reached for Frankie's phone. "How serious is this to the investigation?"

"I would say quite." Frankie nodded at his phone. "Read."

Emma leaned against Abe as they read, both their eyes shooting up to Frankie, and then back down.

"If you are reading this, I am the 'hit woman' hired by Charlie West. I am not a sniper. I am just a woman he found, but that is not all. I will not fulfill this contract. Charlie is responsible for the death of my mother and I want to see him taken down. I will leave evidence that you may not have in a locker at the bus station. If you are agreeable to this, leave word for GS in your local classifieds with just the initials GS and yes. He took too much from me, and I will not allow him to take any more from anyone else."

"Is she for real?" Emma was having trouble digesting what this would mean. Then she was off the couch and over at the desk, sorting through folders until she found the one she wanted, returning to sit beside Abe.

"Here, this is likely her. The initials fit with the daughter - Ginny Smith. She may be using an alias though. Her mother was murdered twelve years ago, around the time Auntie Em was. He was only able to get two million from the estate before the trust fund transferred.”

Frankie reached for the folder. “Do we have this information?”

Emma nodded. “You should have two copies of everything in there. I made sure.”

Frankie nodded. “All right, then. I’ll make sure Jake gets it. Can you add anything to what we’ve found, Emma?”

She shook her head. “I haven’t been allowed on the computer lately, not until at least next week. When I am, it will be limited. So, Jace may be your best bet for information, or Naomi.”

Frankie nodded. “We’ll talk to them, but they’re not as good as you are.”

Emma tilted her head to study Frankie. “Why, Frankie?”

“Why what?”

“The change towards me. Two weeks ago, you were almost accusing me of being a criminal. Now you want to work with me.”

“I had time to think and pray when I was away. I wasn’t fair to you, Emma, or you, Abe. Let's just say God spoke to me and told me off."

Frankie rose, thanked them for the meal, and headed back to the office. He felt the coming end to this but was afraid for his friends.

Chapter 21

Frankie sank into a seat in the conference room beside Jake and nodded at Eddie. He scanned the bustling area and noted the changes on the white board. Jake had moved the investigation forward quite rapidly, he could see.

"Where do we stand with those two men, Jake?"

Jake smiled. "They're wrapping themselves up in so many lies. We've got evidence from other murders and assaults that tie them to Charlie and those incidents. They haven't said where Charlie is though."

"That's a concern," Eddie spoke up. "Given that he no longer has these two, he'll be looking for Abe and Emma. As far as we can tell, they're the only two who were left working for him. When he couldn't pay the others, they left."

"Okay. So, do they know where he's been living?"

Jake shook his head. "No. He never told them, but I would suspect in one of the rundown or abandoned buildings here in town." He sat back, staring at the board. "What did you find out from Abe and Emma?"

"Quite the interesting conversation." Frankie handed over the folder Emma had given him. "Emma thinks this is your lady in the letter."

Jake shot him a quick glance, then looked inside. "Initials match, but that doesn't mean it's her."

"No, it doesn't but it certainly bears further investigation." Eddie reached for the folder. "And I will do that for you, Jake."

Jake nodded. "Thanks, Eddie. Now, Frankie, where do you want to work?"

"I'd like to be in on the search for Charlie, if I may."

Jake nodded, then searched the room. "Talk to Wes. He's been the one coordinating the search." As Frankie moved his chair back to stand, Jake stopped him. "How was Emma?"

"She says she's getting there but can't do any computer work for at least a week, and then only with restrictions. That will be hard for her."

Jake nodded. "Did they ever say anything more about what happened to them?"

Frankie shook his head. "No, they haven't. I think there's something else that went on at that time, but it's between the two of them. They'll tell us if we need to know." Frankie sat for a moment lost in thought. "I still can't fathom how it all happened."

Jake nodded. "I know. This man has such a twisted sense of privilege and entitlement and that everything belongs to him." He looked back as his name was called. "What do you have Bill?"

"I have someone here to talk to an investigator. He says it's to do with Emma's flight ten years ago."

Frankie and Jake stared at each other. "Come on, Frankie. I want you in on this."

Abe stared at Jake and Frankie the next morning. "You said what?"

"We had the man who helped Emma get away ten years ago walk into the department last night." Jake shot a glance at

Frankie. "He has confirmed everything Emma said happened to both you and her."

"I never doubted her word, and I lived through it. So, what makes this so important?"

Frankie spoke up. "He's also got a wealth of documents that tie Charlie to a lot more than being the black widower we know he is. He's got ties to the mob, and that's why they're after him. He's been blackmailing them, and now that they're after him, that line of money is cut off from him."

"So you could end up with a mob war in town, is that what you're saying?"

Frankie nodded. "We could. We just hope it won't." He looked past Abe as Emma hesitated in the doorway. "Emma, I was just about to ask Abe to find you."

"Why? And what brings you out here so early?"

Jake handed her a picture. "Do you recognize this man?"

She took the picture, then her fingers covered her mouth as she nodded. "Jules. He helped me get away." She raised her eyes to them. "Why would you have a picture of him?"

"Because he showed up at the department last night with a whole lot of documents that we now have to work through." Jake shook his head. "Just out of the blue. He saw the PR spot on the news and had to speak up."

"Jules never suited the job he was hired for. I don't think he knew what he was getting into when he hired on. He had only been there about a month when he helped me to escape. Otherwise, I'm sure I would have ended up like Auntie Em." She shuddered at the thought, and Abe wrapped his arms around her. "How does this progress the investigation, Jake?"

"We have people working it through. I have your folder from last night, and we're tracking that lady down. She's in town, all right, she's been seen. We just need to find her."

"I don't think you will. Leave her the message and then she'll leave you the information you want and disappear. If I can make a suggestion, don't try too hard to find her. She's not a sniper. She doesn't even like guns, from what I can read. It was a gunshot that killed her mother."

"That's in the paperwork you gave me?" Frankie studied her face.

"It is, Frankie. I've pulled everything I can on everyone I can find he's had contact with. Some of it has gone on to other police services, but the stacks on the corner of Abe's desk need to go to you." She looked around as she heard the door and saw Joseph and Murphy heading their way through the entry way.

Abe turned. "What brings you two in so early? I thought you were off with your wives for the day."

"We are shortly, Abe," Joseph spoke for the two men. "I just wanted to give you a report on what I found."

Abe nodded, knowing he wasn't going to like what he was to hear.

"They've breached our security on numerous occasions. They've had a security expert on their side, and I can't track down who it is. Micah's been working on that as has Jace." Joseph was both frustrated and angry. "I've made changes, updated our systems, and put in as strong a firewall as I can get. Whoever it is that's hacking in has been good. What I've set up now is a system that if someone tries to hack in, they think they're in, but it directs them to the police department and their IT people, who will track it back."

Abe nodded. "Good work, Joseph. Murphy?"

Murphy took a look at the two detectives, then spoke quietly. "Someone's been around the lake again, Abe. We've found evidence where they'd spent more than one night watching, not close enough that we can spot them."

"Let's bring in a dog or two then, Murphy." Emma searched the faces of the five men. "I know someone who has dogs she'll lend us. That would make a difference at night. One handler would come in with them."

"I'm not sure about bringing in another body here." Abe held up his hands as she went to speak. "Who is it?"

She smiled. "Your friend, Don. One of his men is a dog handler and he has two dogs he's offered us. That's what I was coming to tell you, when I found you with Frankie and Jake."

Abe looked at Murphy over Emma's head. "It's your call, Murphy. You're in charge right now. I'm just the client." Emma dug her elbow into his rib, and he laughed down at her.

Murphy shook his head. "I know who you mean, Emma. Simon does that a lot when he has a chance. I think it might be a good idea to try it."

Frankie and Jake shared a look.

"Sounds like you have things under control here, Murphy." Jake smiled at the married couple glaring at him. "Stay safe, you two. I don't want any more incidents like we just had."

Abe shook his head at Jake and then nodded at Frankie. When the two detectives had left, he turned to Joseph.

"What didn't you say, Joseph? I know there was more."

A grim look came over Joseph face and he looked almost angry. "There is. I've found evidence that the security expert they're using works for the crime lab. I'm heading in to talk with Caleb. He needs to be the one dealing with it. Then Leah and I are off for a couple of days. Stay safe, you two? Please?"

Abe nodded and watched Joseph head out before turning to Murphy. "You're in charge, Murphy, but talk to me."

Murphy pointed at the coffee pot. "I'm putting on a new pot. How be we meet in your office, Abe? Ian's on his way in as well. He's delaying leaving for the day until he talks to you."

Emma sighed as she turned to leave the kitchen. "I want this guy. He's affecting way too many lives."

Abe and Murphy shared a glance, then Abe followed Emma to the office.

"Emma, what's really up?"

She turned, her face pale and weary looking. "I'm tired, Abe. My head still hurts. I can't work. So, what do I do?"

Abe watched as she paced the office. "If I could take you away somewhere until it was over, I would."

She turned. "That might be the best thing, Abe. It sounds as if they're closing in on him. The thing of it is, though, is we don't know who all he has in his pocket."

Murphy handed them each a cup of coffee, then took a seat, also watching Emma pace. "Emma, can you sit for a moment?"

She spun to stare at him, then sat on the couch. "You look so serious this morning, Murphy."

He nodded. "I feel like it's all coming to a head and like a volcano, will erupt at any time. We can't prevent that. Even if they catch him, I think he's put in place a series of events to cover that. He is out to get you, for revenge and retaliation. At this point, he doesn't really care if he's caught or not, as long as you both suffer." He paused to collect his thoughts. "The guys feel the same way. They're wracking their brains in how to keep you two safe."

Emma rose and fetched a paper she had been working on. "That list I put up on the board, Murphy?"

He nodded. "What about it?"

"He's pretty much down to just Nathaniel and Abe. He's covered all the rest of you. Now, if his sniper is really who we suspect, then unless he's hired a second one, that is off the books. That leaves just Abe, as my protector." She turned worried eyes to him. "How is he going to take you out, Abe? That's the question."

Abe nodded. "I know. That's what worries me. We've pretty much confined you to the house, so he can't get to you. I'm back and forth between buildings here. He would have to come down from the rocks."

Murphy nodded. "That's about the only way, unless he gets in during the day when the gates are open, but Joseph has set up the security system to alert if a stranger comes in." He looked between the two. "I think for now, if you're both need to be off site, we have to transport you separately. That means all of us involved, as well as Gideon. Sidney is coming in for the next few days. Don is heading our way. His team is off next week and are adamant they're helping out."

Chapter 22

Charlie stopped short, staring at the building he had been living in, then drew back into a doorway. Red and blue lights flickered across his face. How had they found him? Who sold him out?

He turned, his bag of food clutched in his hands. He needed to find a new place to hole up in, and then find a gun. She would pay for this and so would that husband of hers. Why couldn't he have just stayed dead?

Jake stood in the doorway of the room Charlie had rented. They had heard quite forcefully from the landlord that he was owed weeks of rent that Charlie kept promising him was coming. He was just waiting for a trust fund to come due. He turned to stare back down the hallway, and then back into the room.

Frankie approached from across the room. "It's him all right, Jake. We've found a myriad of documents. But he's not here."

Jake nodded. "I know. I wish he had been. Then this would have been over."

"Not necessarily." Jake turned to Frankie. "If he's set in play a series of commands, then they'll be followed. We have no way of knowing who's working for him now."

Jake mulled this over. "I would expect that he has. Our GS left the key for us and we've retrieved the material she left in the locker. Our team's going over it now. This is turning into a night and day investigation."

"It has. Our fellow police services are working almost as hard as well are proving what Emma forwarded to them."

Jake reached for the evidence bad he was handed. His face paling, he turned to Frankie. "Frankie, this photo was taken today of Abe and Emma. It's date stamped. Once again, it's through their kitchen window. How is he getting these pictures?"

"He has someone else working for him. I would suspect an investigator he's like to." Frankie pulled out his phone. "Gideon? It's Frankie. Jake and I have a question for you. Do you know of an investigator that could get in close to Abe and take photos? Yeah, we got another one through the kitchen window, and it's from today."

He listened as Gideon searched his contacts.

"Here's one. Sidney and I had a run-in with him a couple of years ago. I think Abe did as well. He runs pretty close to the legal line. I've always thought he could easily step over it."

"Thanks, Gideon." Frankie handed Jake the name he had written down.

Jake stopped him. "It's your turn to do this, Frankie. Go get him. I would like to hear what he has to say."

"On it." Frankie looked around, then beckoned to Bill, who was on duty that night. "Bill, just who I want to see. Come on. You're with me. Leave your cruiser keys with someone. We've off to find an investigator."

The investigator gave Frankie a haughty look when Frankie sat down across from him in the interrogation room.

"Why am I here?"

Frankie didn't say anything, just pulled out the two photos and slid them across the table. The man studied them, then raised his eyes.

"What's the meaning of this?"

"We know you took those pictures. We've had a search warrant served on your business and your home. You are now under investigation for attempted murder and assault."

The male paled. "What do you mean? I was asked to take those two photos. That's all."

"That may be all from your standpoint, but it's not from ours when we have two people stalked and almost killed."

His face whitened even more. "I didn't know that. All I was asked to do was take a couple of pictures. Those two pictures." He pointed at them.

Frankie then laid a number of photos of men in front of him, sliding the two other photos back into his folder. "Can you tell me if one of these men is the one who hired you?"

The investigator pointed directly at a photo of Charlie, not even looking at the other ones. "He did. He said he was trying to find evidence of bank fraud, and he suspected these two."

"Did he give you a name to call him?"

"No. He just said to put an ad in the notices in the paper and he'd be in touch. And he never gave me a name for those two."

Frankie sat back, assessing his words. "So, you didn't know that this is Abe Finlay and his wife, Emma?" When he shook his head, Frankie continued, "Just for the record. You didn't know that you were asked to take pictures of Abe Finlay, owner of Rebel's Elite Security, and his wife, Emma Donovan Finlay, owner of Tracker's?"

The man slumped back in his seat and shook his head again. "No. I didn't. He didn't give names."

"And you didn't think it odd that you had to come in over rocks to get to that point to take those pictures? You didn't think it odd all those buildings around there?"

The man shook his head. "No. I've been asked before to take photos similar to this." He stopped. "You know, he sounds like a client I had before." He went on to give details, Frankie knowing that Jake and Eddie were listening.

Eddie turned to Jake. "We've got him, if we can ever find him."

Jake was frustrated. "I know. He's gone underground, and none of our sources are saying anything."

Eddie looked past Jake as the door opened. "Ben Johnson! What are you doing here?" Ben was a retired detective and good friend to Eddie

"If I could talk to you two for a moment? I'm told Frankie's tied up with an interrogation."

Ben followed Jake to his office. What he had to share would shake up the investigation in a way he never thought possible.

"Ben, you're troubled. For you to come in looking for us at this time of night, it has to be serious."

Ben sighed, then nodded. "You know me well, Eddie. We worked together for so many years. I was given information tonight that will affect your investigation. It comes from an anonymous source but is easily verifiable. Jace is working on that for me." He stopped, gathering his words.

"Emma's father was a computer programmer. The shares she gave away were from his company. I have learned that one of his employees is involved in your investigation as well. Charlie is not the only one after her. This person feels that they were cheated by her father. She's been tracking Emma for years, losing her when Emma ran from her home. It was just a fluke that she found her a few months ago. She's the one who hired the sniper that went after Nathaniel. She's the one who has been targeting Abe's men. She's knew Emma and Abe were married and has been watching Abe, trying to find Emma."

Jake and Eddie sat back. This put a whole new light on the investigation. "There's more than one involved?"

Ben nodded. He handed over a pile of papers he had been holding. "This is the research I've been able to come up with." He looked up. "And here's Jace with more."

"That right, Ben. Jake, Ben asked me to search for this lady. She's here in town. What you're not going to like is that she is a cousin to one of your lab techs, the one who researches your security systems."

Frankie and Jake shared a look. "Joseph was right. He warned us to look into that."

"I'll go talk with Joseph." Eddie stood, then looked at the clock. "No, he's to be away for a couple of days, he said. I guess that will be Murphy then I'm talking to in the morning." He sat back down, then reached for the material Ben had brought in, scanning it. "Ben, did you notice this?"

Ben nodded. "I did. I have a good idea who that man is, but I can't say."

Eddie nodded. "I think you're right." He sighed. "How many undercover officers do we have in the downtown area now?"

Jake looked at them, not quite following their conversation. "I think five or six. Why?"

"Because the information seems to be coming from one of them. We can't verify unless we come up with a reason to arrest him or her."

Jake shook his head. "This is just getting more and more complicated." He looked up as Frankie appeared in the doorway. "All done?"

Frankie nodded. "He caved when he realized what he was facing. I have an officer taking his statement. What's I just overheard?"

Eddie handed him the folder and Ben's paperwork. "Just to get you up to speed, Charlie's not the one who hired the sniper. It's a former employee of Emma's father."

Frankie stared at Eddie, then down at the paperwork he held. "Now, why can't we just have a nice simple straight investigation? What is it with Abe and his guys, throwing a monkey wrench into the investigations all the time?" He pointed at Jake. "I'm not the one talking to him this time."

The other men laughed at his words. "No, Frankie, I will be." Eddie stood. "I'm off for home. I need to catch a few hours of sleep. Coming, Ben?"

Chapter 23

Abe paced the kitchen of his home, waiting for Emma to come down. It was Sunday and they would be leaving for church shortly. He knew his guys' ladies had gone on ahead, carpooling together. His men were pacing outside, waiting for them. He turned as he heard Emma coming towards him.

"Abe, I'm not sure about this. It's putting so many people at risk." Emma rubbed her arms with her hands.

"We need to be in church, Emma. Please look at me. We have to have that communion with our friends and church family. We need to be in God's presence. Yes, we can do that here, but today, I just need to be there."

She nodded. "Well, then, I guess we go. But you said we're not riding together?"

Abe shook his head, looking up as Murphy entered. "No. The guys want us in separate vehicles."

She turned to face Murphy. "Then, who I am riding with?"

"Nathaniel, Ian, Luke and Micah. Gideon's riding with us, Abe."

Emma could see his weapon as he turned, his jacket brushing it. She paled. "I want this over, Murphy, and today isn't soon enough."

"I know, Emma. Go on. They're waiting for you."

Abe kissed her, then watched as she walked away. "That's not all, is it, Murphy?"

He shook his head. "No, Eddie's will be speaking with you today. Ben found evidence that Charlie didn't hire the sniper. A disgruntled employee from Emma's father's company did. This woman's been tracking her for years. From what we can determine, she's been the one sending the warning letters all along, and the one who hired the sniper who went after Nathaniel, and the one who hired all those other guys that went after us."

Abe stared at him. "Really? It's credible, Ben's information? Then that changes everything. Let's go. I want to find Emma."

Eddie slid into the pew beside Abe. "I need to talk to you two today. I'll be out this afternoon."

Abe nodded, then turned as Emma touched his arm. "What's that about, Abe?"

"Murphy let me know that Charlie isn't the one who's been trying to kill us, at least not the only one. They're trying to verify the identity of the other one. They think she's the one who hired the sniper, not Charlie."

Emma nodded, a thoughtful look on her face. "That's what been wrong all along, Abe. Charlie doesn't have the mentality or the personality to hire a sniper. That's what I couldn't figure out. You say Eddie's coming out this afternoon?"

"He is. I imagine Jake or Frankie will be with him."

They settled back to listen to Greg's message on God's protection, how one could never know what they had been protected from, and how God provided protection. Emma was lost in thought as the service ended.

"Abe, Emma. We need you two to wait inside until we get the vehicles in place. We're going out the back door." Murphy stood beside them, eyes scanning the area around them. "We're heading for the police department instead of home. Jake wants to meet us there."

Emma waited for Micah to open her door at the station. They were in the back lot, planning of walking in the back door. Sudden gunfire rang out, and Micah slammed the door as he dove back into the vehicle.

"Move us out, Ian."

Emma turned, searching for Abe's vehicle. "It's not moving, Micah. Why not?" Her face grew anxious as her heart fell.

Micah's phone chimed, and he answered, his eyes sliding to Emma, then back out the window.

"Murphy wants us to hold steady right here, Ian."

"Micah, what's going on? Is Abe okay?"

Micah's eyes met the other three men's and they read the answer there.

"Emma, Murphy said Abe was hit. He doesn't know how bad yet."

"Abe shot?" She tried to push past Micah and then Luke. "I need to get to him."

Micah's hand gripped her arms. "No, we need you to stay inside here. You're not safe."

"Like Abe was safe in a police parking lot? Let me by, Micah."

Micah shook his head, his back planted to the door.

Abe had turned to search for Emma when his body slammed into Matt, taking them both to the ground. Murphy dropped to his knees beside Abe, who was sprawled on the pavement, face down. Matt had risen to his knees and was working to stem the flow of blood.

"Are the paramedics on their way, Jake?" Murphy's voice raised above the confusion in the lot.

"They're here. We're just clearing it out so they can get in." Jake turned as his name was called.

"Up on that roof, Jake. That's where the sniper is. I can still see their form." Doug's team had been in the building and his sniper was watching where the sniper was. A sudden movement, a shot rang out, and the sniper's rifle clattered on the pavement. Doug's team moved out.

Dave dropped to his knees beside Matt, paramedic and good friend to Abe. "Where's he shot?"

"His back. It's near the spine, Dave, so we'll need to be careful. We didn't see anyone, and we were looking."

Dave nodded, then spoke with his partner, Tom, who headed back for the Stryker board. "We'll transport him on the board, Matt. Jake, do we have an escort?"

"They're lining up to provide one, Dave. Our men and women are angry."

Dave nodded. "Okay, let's get on our way. Where's Emma?"

"She's in our other vehicle." Murphy looked around. "We had them split up today to come to town. I didn't want them to, but Abe insisted he had to be in church."

Dave nodded as he helped lift Abe to the stretcher. "Let's roll, Tom. Who's with us?"

"Joseph and Matt." Murphy turned as Eddie approached.

"I just heard it was Abe. How is he?" Eddie's face was white with shock.

"I'm not sure, Eddie." He caught Eddie's arm as he swayed. "Dave's on his way in with him right now. Ride in with us."

Emma paced the waiting room, exhausted but her nerves were too pent up for her to sit. Abe's teams watched her, and then the people surrounding her.

"We'll need to find a room we can put her in soon, Murphy." Nathaniel studied the growing number of officers who were appearing. "You would think it was one of the officers who had been hurt."

"Abe's father was well liked in town. When he set up his security business with his brother, he made sure he worked with the police service. Abe continued that. Abe's liked for who his father was and for who he is." Murphy turned as Emma approached him, reaching out to hug her.

"No word yet, Murphy. Why won't they come talk to me?"

Murphy's eyes lifted to see John Thompson walking slowly towards them, a stern look on his face. Murphy's heart sank. No, please Lord, let him be alive.

"Emma?" John touched her arm, causing her to jump. "Come with me. I'm taking you to a room where we can speak quietly. I think Murphy would like to get you out of being in the open." Murphy nodded.

Emma searched the room, looking for Rebecca. "Rebecca's not here, Murphy. Where is she?"

"I think she and Gideon are on their way in. Gideon had gone to get her." Murphy beckoned for the team to follow. Before following Emma into the room, he had a quiet word with them, and they spread out to provide the security they knew was needed, hearts lifting in prayer for their friends.

"Emma, sit please." John waited for her to sit, then pulled a chair up in front of her. "So, this is where we stand. Abe is very lucky or should I say, God had His hand on him today. He's alive. He was shot in the back, the bullet entering near the spine but deflecting down off a rib. We'll need to take him to surgery to repair the damage, but from what I'm seeing there's not a lot of internal damage. We're concerned though about how close the bullet was to the spine."

"Is he paralyzed?" Emma's voice was barely audible.

"We don't know that yet, Emma. It may be he is on a temporary basis or on a permanent basis or not at all." He looked up at Murphy. "I need to get back to him. Give us a few minutes, then a nurse will come find you. You can ride up to the surgical floor with him when we take him up. We're waiting for the on-call surgeon to arrive."

Emma nodded. "Murphy, when Rebecca gets in, please bring her to me? I want her with me."

Murphy nodded, his eyes on Emma's face. It was set in a stone-like mask, her eyes not even seeming alive.

Murphy watched as Emma sat, unmoving, in a chair near the corner of the surgical waiting room. She had been there since Abe had been taken to surgery and she had been unable to see him before that. Murphy turned as Eddie and Peg entered.

"She's just sitting there, Murphy?" Peg's voice was quiet and full of concern.

"She is, Peg. She hasn't moved at all."

"She's reliving ten years ago, Murphy. I understand she didn't get to see him before they brought him to surgery?"

Murphy shook his head. "And she should have. Given their history, she should have." Murphy was frustrated.

Peg and Eddie moved to sit on either side of Emma, Peg reached for her hand.

Emma slowly shook off the fog she was in and heard the voices speaking to her. She turned and saw Eddie's concerned face.

"Eddie!" She searched the room. "There's been no word?"

Eddie shook his head. "It's early yet, Emma." He watched her face. "He's alive, my dear, and coming back to you. It's not like ten years ago."

Her eyes flew to his compassionate ones, and her stillness and resolve broke. He reached to draw her into his arms, just as he would his daughter had she lived and faced something like this. Peg's hand rubbed Emma's back as she wept.

Finally, raising her face, Emma touched Eddie's shirt. "I've soaked your shirt, Eddie. I'm sorry."

He shook his head. "Not a problem, Emma. Never a problem. You've needed this." He shared a look with his wife.

Emma looked over as she heard people talking at the door and saw Dr. Johns heading her way.

"Amos! Please, tell me he's still alive!"

Amos crouched down in front of her and reached for her hands. "He is, Emma. He's strong and a fighter. The damage was not as bad as we first thought. Nothing internal. There may be some residual nerve damage, but I don't expect that to be a problem." He looked up at Eddie and then Peg. "He's in recovery right now. We'll come get you when we move him to a room, likely in a couple of hours."

Emma nodded. "I want to stay with him, Amos. I can't leave him." Tears found their way to the surface again.

Amos had heard their story from John and readily agreed.

Murphy watched Emma relax against the back of her seat and nod as Eddie spoke to her.

Eddie rose and headed for Murphy. "It's good news, Murphy. No internal injuries. No paralysis."

Murphy's eyes slid shut as he breathed a prayer of thanks. He could hear the murmurs from behind him as the other team members heard the news.

"Emma's planning on staying with him."

Emma's eyes were heavy and she fought to stay awake. Peg watched her, then nodded.

"Emma?" She waited until Emma turned to her. "Are you okay?"

Emma nodded. "I think I finally am. Abe and I have had to deal with something that happened ten years ago." She hesitated, then made a decision. "Neither of us have parents left to serve as grandparents for our children. I would be honoured if you and Eddie would step in, just as you have as parents to Abe and Rebecca."

Peg, reading the news in Emma's face, nodded, then reached to hug her. "We would be delighted to, my dear. You've become a special part of our family, a long time joining us, though."

Emma giggled, then looked up as Ian approached.

"Emma, I have a young man here who wants to speak with you."

Emma peered around him. "Tony? What's he doing here?"

Ian shrugged. "He just asked if he could speak with you." He turned and motioned Tony over, stepping back but not far away.

Tony sat where Eddie had been and studied Emma. "You've been through a lot, Emma. But Dad got word this morning that Charlie is dead." He held out a piece of paper to her. "Dad doesn't have a lot of details, but it seems the people Charlie was borrowing money from wanted it back and he didn't have it to give."

Emma's hand stopped as she reached for the paper. "I'm glad your Dad is no longer part of that group, Tony."

Tony stood, staring into the distance, then looking down at Emma. "If you hadn't come into our lives, Emma, I would not have my parents or my sisters in my life. We would never again have been a family or found God. Thank you." He reached down to kiss her, then turned and walked away, the men's eyes following him.

Emma searched for Eddie, rising to go find him. "Eddie, Tony gave me this. I think you'll find Charlie's body here. I know you had word he was dead."

"We did, Emma. Thank you." Eddie was reluctant to leave but knew he had to. "Call me when you see Abe, please, Emma?"

"I will." She reached to hug him and whispered. "I asked Peg to be our honorary grandmother. Will you do the same as a grandfather?"

Eddie stilled, then leaned back to look in her face, reading the message she wouldn't put into words yet. He hugged her back.

Emma watched her husband's face as he roused, the stubble on it rough under her touch. God, You have been so good. You brought my love back to me and have blessed me with so many new friends and family.

Abe's eyes fluttered open and closed. He knew Emma was standing beside him, but he couldn't rouse enough to speak to her.

Emma turned as the door open and a nurse entered. She frowned. This was not the nurse Dr. Johns had assigned to them.

"I'm sorry, you have the wrong room." Emma's voice was forceful.

The woman shook her head. "No, it's the right room. And for once, you're where I can find you."

Emma studied her. "I'm sorry. I don't know you."

"You should. Your father stole from me."

Emma shook her head, not understanding.

"I was with your father's company for ten years and was due to get my shares. Instead, he had to go overseas and get killed. You shut down the company before I got my shares. You owe me."

Emma's eyes stayed steady on the woman as she pulled out a knife. "I'm sorry, but Dad had stopped the shares a year before he was killed. Didn't you know that?"

"That's a lie!" The woman leapt for Emma but was stopped in her forward movement as Murphy and Micah wrapped hands around her arms.

"That's not happening, lady." They pushed her back out of the room and into Jake's hands.

Jake had appeared at the hospital, having had word that the woman was there.

"Thanks, fellows. I think this is it now." He eyed Emma as she stood at the door. "We've got them all now, Emma. She was the last. Just need to wrap up everything in a nice little package for the prosecutor. Thank you and Jace for all your help."

Emma nodded, watching as he walked away. "Go home, fellows. It's over. Go spend time with your ladies. I'll call if I need anything." She turned, letting the door close behind her.

Abe roused once again as he sensed Emma near him and turned, meeting her tear-streaked face.

"Emma?"

"It's over, Abe. It's finally over. They have them all, and what a story we have to talk about."

Abe grimaced as he reached for Emma and pulled her down to him. "It doesn't matter, sweetheart. Just so long as you are unhurt and with me."

Eight months later, Abe perched on a railing on his back deck and watched the crowd mingling in his back yard. His team members and their wives were there. Eddie and Peg, Caleb and Hannah, Gideon and Rebecca. He knew others had wanted to be there but couldn't.

He felt Emma's arms slip around his waist and he hugged her to him.

"It's such a great group, Abe." Emma was content. "Did you see Caleb with his little daughter?"

Abe laughed. "He's always wanted a daughter to spoil. Now he has a three month old. I pity the guys that take an interest in her."

Emma laughed, then searched for Peg. Peg had taken their little son, Isaac Peter, from her earlier and had not put him down. "Peg and Eddie are really taking on the roles of grandparents."

"They are. I am so glad you asked that of them."

Emma shrugged, her eyes following the women in the group. "You know, we're going to need to put in a playground here."

Abe nodded, his eyes moving towards the lake. "The new training facility is almost finished. That will free up this area just to be our homes."

Emma nodded. "I'm glad, Abe. It's time we moved on to that." She tilted her head back to look up at him. "I never thought that I would be part of such a group. God has provided for us in so many ways. His protection over our adventure, as Frankie calls it, kept us alive, even though we were hurt."

"God knew what He was doing, Emma. Murphy's favourite saying is that God has a plan and purpose we don't know about."

"He does at that." Content to be held, Emma's thoughts flew over the past few years. God had indeed been good.

"Have you thought of a name for your town yet, Abe?"

He shot her a look, then started laughing. "I would say The Haven."

"I like that. It's what it has become for all of us. A haven and a port in times of trouble."

Dear Readers:

Thank you for picking up the story of Abe and his lady Emma. It's the last in the His Guardians series. How did Emma and Abe protect their hearts? Abe went silent, keeping it all locked inside. Emma locked down herself and became determined to make sure no one else suffered as she had. She refused to let herself feel emotions.

Once again, the story wrote itself. Nothing was really planned, other than the letters and incidents with the other seven men and their ladies, leading up to the story of Abe and Emma.

How does God protect us? In so many ways, He does. We often don't know or see how He does. He is our refuge, the rock we run to, our strong tower in times of need. As an example, as a teenager walking home from school or work, on three different occasions, a dog walked me to my dog. Three different dogs that I had never seen before or never saw again. To me, that was God's protection on those days.

I will miss these men and their ladies. They have become a part of my life. I never knew what adventure they'd end up in or how God would work. Matt and his Sarah, Nathaniel and his Elizabeth, Murphy and his

Adriel, Ian and his Lydia, Joseph and his Leah, Luke and his Abigail, Micah and his Kataleen, and of course Abe and his Emma. I knew the men's names but the ladies' names usually developed as I went to write the stories. The ladies' occupations did the same. Why have a lady as a secretary or a nurse or whatever is usually thought of as a female occupation? I had to put some fun into the stories.

The animals in the stories are based on mine. I have three Shetland Sheepdogs (Shelties) - Emma, Liam, and Natalie - from a wonderful breeder friend, Heather Walton of Aberdale Shelties. She is the one who risked her life on a busy highway to rescue a little six-week-old gray tabby, who became my Ceilidh. My tuxedo cat, Ciara, really does sleep on me. Ceilidh doesn't meow or even purr much, hence Meow Too. The flowers on the covers - from my garden, a passion I shared with my Mom.

God bless each one of you who have chosen to read this series. May the words God wrote through me (and each story is from Him) be a blessing and a challenge to each one of you.

Look for more stories upcoming. I have a list of ideas. My Under His Wings trilogy, The Haven of Rest Trilogy and the

standalone story of Doug and his Darcy were
also all written as God directed.

Blessings

Ronna